Dear Reader,

Joe Mackenzie was sp

he stepped into a scene in *Mackenzie's Mountain,* a book about his father, Wolf. I received hundreds of letters asking for Joe's story, and even though it has been several years since his book was published, I still get letters about him.

Silhouette is reprinting Joe's book, *Mackenzie's Mission,* as part of their 20th Anniversary celebration. The last Mackenzie book, *A Game of Chance,* will be on sale in August of 2000.

This family has captured readers' imaginations far beyond anything I ever imagined. With each successive book about them (*Mackenzie's Pleasure, Mackenzie's Magic*), the letters have increased. Thank each and every one of you who has taken the time to write and express your love of this family. The Mackenzies are special to me, too. If you haven't had the opportunity to read Joe's story before, I hope you enjoy it.

Sincerely,

Linda Howard

LINDA HOWARD

"Ms. Howard can wring so much emotion and tension out of her characters that no matter how satisfied you are when you finish a book, you still want more."
—*Rendezvous Magazine*

"Howard's writing is compelling."
—*Publishers Weekly*

"Linda Howard is an extraordinary talent whose unforgettable novels are richly flavored with scintillating sensuality and high-voltage suspense."
—*Romantic Times Magazine*

"You can't just read one Linda Howard!"
—Catherine Coulter,
New York Times bestselling author

"Already a legend in her own time, Linda Howard exemplifies the very best of the romance genre. Her strong characterizations and powerful insight into the human heart have made her an author cherished by readers everywhere."
—Melinda Helfer, *Romantic Times Magazine*

"Linda Howard writes with power, stunning sensuality and a storytelling ability unmatched in the romance genre. Every book is a treasure for the reader to savor again and again."
—Iris Johansen,
New York Times bestselling author

LINDA HOWARD

MACKENZIE'S MISSION

Silhouette® Books

Published by Silhouette Books
America's Publisher of Contemporary Romance

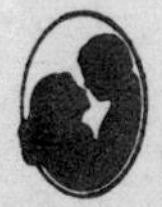

SILHOUETTE BOOKS

MACKENZIE'S MISSION

ISBN 0-373-48408-9

This edition published by arrangement with Harlequin Books S.A.

Visit Silhouette at www.eHarlequin.com

Printed in U.S.A.

MACKENZIE FAMILY TREE

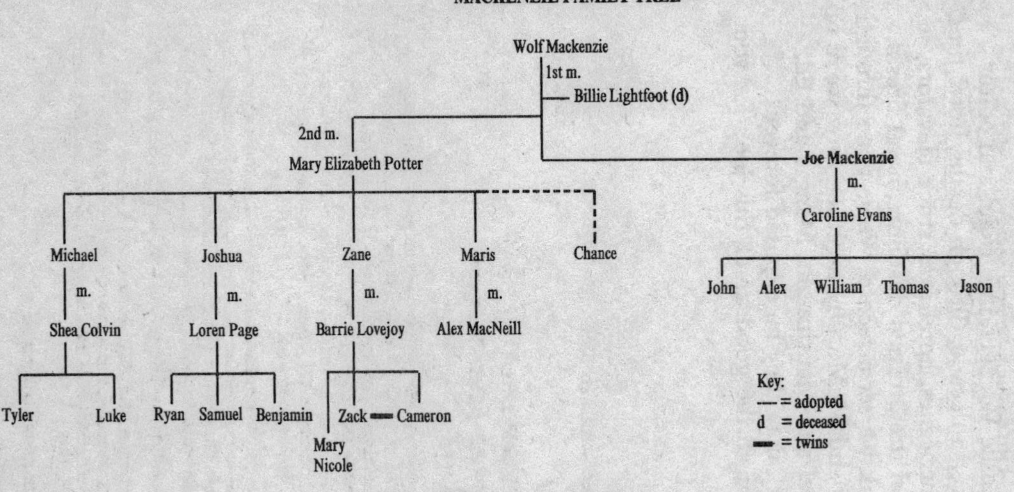

Look for A Game of Chance, *featuring Chance Mackenzie, available in August from Silhouette Intimate Moments!*

Leslie Wainger, my friend and editor
for over a decade, through deaths, hotel fires,
hurricanes, hotel fires, stuck elevators,
hotel fires, missed deadlines, hotel fires....
I think we set a record. We've gone through
Sonny and McMurphy together, now we're on
Joel and Maurice and Maggie and Ed,
may they be exposed forever.
So for all the good times, this Joe's for you.

Prologue

"Man must be trained for war, and woman for the relaxation of the warriors; all else is folly."
—Friedrich Nietsche

"Hogwash." *—Linda Howard*

He was a legend even before he graduated from the Academy, at least among his own classmates and the underclassmen. As first in his graduating class he had his pick of assignments, and to no one's surprise, he chose fighter jets. The politically savvy all knew that the fastest way to promotion in the Air Force was as an aviator, and fighter wings, with their inherent glamour, had always been the most visible. But those who knew Joe Mackenzie, newly commissioned officer in the United States Air Force, knew he didn't give a damn about promotion, only about flying.

His superiors had doubts about his suitability for fighters, but that was the training he had chosen, and they decided to give him the opportunity. He was six foot three, almost too tall for a fighter jockey. He'd be okay as a bomber pilot, but the dimensions of the cockpit in a fighter meant it would be a tight fit for him, and the physical demands of G forces were generally better met by men who were less than six feet tall, and of stockier build. Of course, there were exceptions to every rule, and the statistics for the physical build of the best fighter pilots were general profiles, not hard-and-fast rules. So Joe Mackenzie was given his chance at fighter training.

His training instructors found that, despite his height, he was better than competent: he was superb. He was that once-in-a-lifetime jet jockey, the one who set the standards for everyone who came after him. He was peculiarly suited, both physically and mentally, for the job he had chosen. His eyesight was better than twenty-twenty, his reflexes were phenomenal and his cardiovascular condition was so good that he was able to withstand greater G forces than his shorter fellow trainees. He remained at the top in his classes on physics and aerodynamics. He had a light touch with the controls and was willing to spend extra hours in the flight simulator perfecting his skills. Most of all, he had the unteachable quality of "situation awareness," the ability to be aware of everything going on around him in a fluid situation and adjust his actions accordingly. All aviators had to have it to some degree, but only in the best of them was it highly developed. He had an amazing degree of it. By the time Joe Mackenzie earned his wings, he was already known as a "hot stick," one of those with the magic touch.

As a very young captain in the first Gulf War, he downed three enemy aircraft in *one day,* an achievement that, to his relief, wasn't publicized. The reasons for it were political: to ensure better public relations with their allies, the United States Air Force was willing to let pilots from the other countries get the glory. Captain Mackenzie was more than willing to go along with policy. It had been mere chance, on the second day of the war, that had put him in the middle of the toughest resistance the enemy put up during the short length of the hostilities. He hadn't been impressed with the enemy pilots' skills. Nevertheless, for about three minutes it had been a real fur ball, when he and his wingman had been jumped by six enemy fighters.

The end result was an almost indecently fast promotion to Major, and Joe Mackenzie, tactical call sign "Breed," was recognized as the fastest of the fast trackers, a fast-burner on his way to a general's star.

During the second Gulf War, Major Mackenzie scored two more official kills in air-to-air combat and was designated an ace. This time there was no way to keep his achievements out of the media, not that the Pentagon wanted to; it recognized that it had a public-relations gold mine in the handsome half-breed American Indian, who exemplified all of the qualities they most wanted to project. He was given the choice assignments and made lieutenant colonel at the age of thirty-two. It was generally recognized that for Breed Mackenzie, there was nowhere to go but up.

Chapter 1

She was the most beautiful bitch he'd ever seen, fast and sleek and deadly. Just looking at her made his heart beat faster. Even parked in the hangar, her engines cold and wheels chocked, she gave the impression of pure speed.

Colonel Joe Mackenzie reached out and touched the fuselage, his long fingers caressing her with the light touch of a lover. The dark metallic skin of her airframe had a slick feel to it that was different from every other fighter he'd flown, and the difference entranced him. He knew it was because her airframe was a revolutionary new composite of thermoplastics, graphite and industrial spider silk, which was far stronger and more flexible than steel, meaning she could withstand far greater force without breaking apart than any aircraft ever before built. Intellectually he knew that, but emotionally he felt that it was because she was so alive. She didn't feel quite like metal; maybe it was the spider silk, but she wasn't as cold to the touch as any other airplane.

Developmental programs were usually given code names that didn't reflect the program's nature, which was why the earlier SR-71 Blackbird had been code named "Oxcart." This particular bird, a second-generation advanced tactical fighter, bore the unusually descriptive code name of Night Wing, and when it went into production it would receive some suitably macho designation like the F-15 Eagle or the F-16 Fighting Falcon, but to Colonel Mackenzie she was "Baby." There were actually five prototypes, and he called them all Baby. The test pilots assigned to the program under his command complained that she—whichever "she" it was—always acted up with them because he had spoiled her for other pilots. Colonel Mackenzie had given them his legendary ice-blue stare and replied, "That's what all my women say." His face had remained perfectly expressionless, leaving his men uncertain if that was the truth or a joke. They suspected it to be the truth.

Joe Mackenzie had flown a lot of hot planes, but Baby was special, not just in her construction and power, but her weapons system. She was truly revolutionary, and she was his; as program manager, it was his responsibility to get the kinks worked out of her so she could go into full production. That was assuming Congress came through with the funding, but General Ramey was confident that there wouldn't be any problem there. For one thing, the manufacturer had brought her in on budget, unlike the overrun fiasco that had killed the A-12 in the last decade.

For a long time stealth technology had detracted from a fighter plane's agility and power, until the advent of supercruise had alleviated some of the power problems. Baby was both stealthy and agile, with vectored thrust that let her turn tighter than any fighter had ever turned before, and at higher speeds. She supercruised at Mach 2, and broke Mach 3 in afterburner. And her weapons system used adjustable laser firing, ALF, a mild little acronym for what would someday revolutionize warfare. Mackenzie knew he was involved in the making of history. Lasers had been used for targeting for some time, the beam guiding missiles to the selected location, but for the first time lasers were being used as the weapons themselves. Scientists had finally solved the difficulty of a manageable energy source for X-ray lasers and teamed it with sophisticated optics. Sensors in the pilot's helmet allowed him to spot a missile, target or enemy plane *in any direction,* and the adjustable targeting system followed the direction of the sensors in the helmet. No matter how an enemy plane turned and juked it couldn't escape; a target would have to go faster than the speed of light to escape the laser beam, something not likely to happen.

Baby was so complex that only the best of the best had been assigned to this phase of her development, and the security surrounding her was so tight that an ant would have had a hard time getting into the hangar without proper clearance.

"Anything you need, sir?"

Joe turned, shifting his attention to Staff Sergeant Dennis Whiteside, known as "Whitey," who possessed fiery red hair, a multitude of freckles and a mechanical genius that bordered on miraculous where airplanes were concerned. Whitey considered Baby *his* plane and suffered the pilots touching her only because he couldn't figure out a way to prevent it.

"Just checking her over before I turn in," Joe replied. "Weren't you supposed to go off duty hours ago?"

Whitey took a rag from his back pocket and gently polished the spot where Joe's fingers had touched the plane. "There were some things I wanted to make sure were done right," he replied. "You're taking her up in the morning, aren't you, sir?"

"Yes."

Whitey grunted. "At least you don't jerk her around the way some of those guys do," he said grouchily.

"If you notice any of my guys treating any of the birds rough, let me know."

"Well, it ain't rough, exactly. It's just that they don't have your touch."

"All the same, I mean what I said."

"Yes, sir."

Joe clapped Whitey on the shoulder and headed for his quarters. The sergeant stared after him for a long minute. He had no doubt that the colonel would indeed make any pilot pray he would die and go to hell just to escape his wrath if any of them were caught being careless or stupid with any of the Night Wing prototypes. Colonel Mackenzie was notorious for accepting nothing less than perfection from his pilots, but at the same time they all knew that he valued his men's lives above all else, and maintenance on the birds had to be top-notch, which was why Whitey was still in the hangar long after he should have been off duty. Mackenzie demanded the best from everyone in this program, with no exceptions. A mistake in maintenance on the ground could lead to the loss of one of these eighty-million-dollar aircraft, or even the death of a pilot. It wasn't a job for anyone with a casual attitude.

As Joe walked through the desert night he saw a light on in one of the offices and turned his steps toward the metal building. He didn't object to people working late, but he wanted everyone to be awake and alert the next day, too. There were some workaholics assigned to the Night Wing project who would work eighteen hours a day if he didn't ride herd on them.

His steps were silent, not because he was trying to sneak up on anyone but because that was how he'd been taught to walk from the time he'd taken his first step. Not that anyone in the offices would have heard him approaching anyway; the air conditioners were humming, trying to offset the late July heat and never quite succeeding. The metal Quonset huts seemed to absorb the blistering sun.

The building was dark except for the light in a cubicle on the left. It was one of the offices used by the civilian laser-targeting team, working on-site to troubleshoot the glitches that inevitably showed up when a new system was put into operation. Joe remembered that a new technician had been scheduled to arrive that day, to replace one of the original team who had had a slight heart attack a week before. The guy who'd had the attack was doing okay, but his doctor didn't want him working in the hundred-degree-plus heat, so the company had flown in a replacement.

Joe was curious about the replacement, a woman named Caroline Evans. He'd heard the other three members of the team grousing about her, calling her "the Beauty Queen," and their tone hadn't been admiring. The team might be civilian, but he couldn't allow friction within the group to affect their work. If everyone couldn't get along, he would have to tell the laser-systems people to replace their replacement. He wanted to talk to whichever of the team was working late, find out if Ms. Evans had arrived without incident and exactly what the problem was that they didn't want to work with her.

He walked silently up to the open doorway and stood in it for a minute, watching. The woman in the office had to be the Beauty Queen herself, because she sure as hell wasn't anyone he'd ever met before. He would have remembered if he had.

It wasn't any hardship to watch her, that was for certain. His erect posture slowly stiffened as every muscle in his body surged to alert status. He'd been tired, but suddenly adrenaline was humming through his system and all of his senses became acute, just the way they did when he kicked in the afterburners and went ballistic.

She wore a straight red skirt that ended well above

her knees. Her shoes were off, and she was leaning back in her chair, her bare feet propped on the desk. Joe leaned his shoulder against the door frame, leisurely surveying the smooth, curved legs that had been exposed. No stockings; the heat made them impractical. Nice legs. Better than nice. Verging on stupendous.

A sheaf of computer printouts were on her lap, and she was checking each item, referring occasionally to a textbook beside her. A cup of pale green tea was gently steaming within easy reach of her often blindly reaching hand. Her hair was a pale, bell-shaped curve, combed straight back from her face in the classic style and just long enough to bounce on her shoulders. He could see only part of her face, enough to note her high cheekbones and full lips.

Suddenly he wanted her to face him. He wanted to see her eyes, hear her voice.

"Time to shut it down for the night," he said.

She shot up from the chair with a stifled shriek, tea spilling in one direction and the computer printout in another, long legs flying as she brought them down to the floor, the chair sent spinning across the room to crash into the filing cabinets. She whirled to face him, one hand pressed to her breast as if she could physically calm her heartbeat. A very shapely breast, he noticed, for her hand had pulled the fabric of her cotton blouse tight across her flesh.

Anger flashed like lightning across her face, then was just as suddenly gone as her eyes widened. "Oh my God," she said in a hushed tone. "It's G.I. Joe."

He caught the subtle undertone of sarcasm, and his black eyebrows lifted. "*Colonel* G.I. Joe."

"So I see," she said admiringly. "A full bird colonel. And a ring-knocker," she added, pointing to his academy ring and using the less than complimentary term for an academy graduate. "Either you mugged a colonel and stole his insignia, had a fantastic face-lift and dyed your hair black, or you have a sponsor with some heavy-duty juice who's rushing you through the grades."

He kept his expression bland. "Maybe I'm damn good at what I do."

"Promotion on merit?" she asked, as if it were a concept so impossible it was beyond consideration. "Naahh."

He was accustomed to women reacting to him in varying ways, ranging from fascination to a certain intimidation that bordered on fear, always based on a very physical awareness of him. He was also used to commanding respect, if not liking. None of that was in Caroline Evans' expression. She hadn't taken her eyes off him for a second, her gaze as steady and piercing as a gunslinger's. Yeah, that was it; she was facing him like an adversary.

He straightened away from the door frame and held out his hand, abruptly deciding to put the situation on a professional standing and let her know who she was dealing with. "Colonel Joe Mackenzie, project manager." Service protocol stated that shaking hands was a woman's choice, that a male officer should never extend his hand to a woman first, but he wanted to feel her hand in his and sensed that if he gave her the option, even that touch wouldn't be allowed.

She didn't hesitate but firmly clasped his hand. "Caroline Evans, replacement for Boyce Walton on the laser team." Two quick up and down pumps, then she withdrew her hand.

Since she was barefoot, he could accurately estimate her height as around five-four; the top of her head was even with his collarbone. The difference in their sizes didn't intimidate her, even though she had to look up to meet his gaze. Her eyes were a dark green, he saw, framed by dark lashes and brows that suggested the gold of her hair was chemically achieved.

He nodded toward the printout on the floor. "Why are you working so late, especially on your first day on the job? Is anything wrong that I need to know about?"

"Not that I know of," she replied, stooping down to pick up the accordion of paper. "I was just double-checking some items."

"Why? What made you think of it?"

She gave him an impatient look. "I'm a chronic double-checker. I always double-check that the oven is off, the iron unplugged, the door locked. I look both ways *twice* before I cross a road."

"You haven't found anything wrong?"

"No, of course not. I've already said so."

He relaxed once he was assured that nothing was wrong with the targeting system and resumed his leisurely and enjoyable survey of Caroline Evans as she took a roll of paper towels from a desk drawer and used a couple of sheets to blot up the spilled tea. She bent and twisted with a fluid ease that struck him as sexy. Everything she had done so far, even the barely veiled challenge of her gaze, had struck him as sexy. His loins tightened in response.

She tossed the wet paper towels in the trash and slipped her feet into her shoes. "Nice meeting you, Colonel," she said without looking at him. "See you tomorrow."

"I'll walk you to your quarters."

"No thanks."

The immediate, casual dismissal of his offer irritated him. "It's late, and you're alone. I'm walking you to your quarters."

She did look at him then, turning to face him and putting her hands on her hips. "I appreciate the offer, Colonel, but I don't need those kinds of favors."

"*Those kinds* of favors? What kind are we talking about?"

"The kind that do more harm than good. Look, you're the head honcho. If anyone sees you walking me to my quarters, within two days I'll be hearing snide comments about how I wouldn't be on the team if I wasn't playing footsie with you. It's a hassle I can do without."

"Ah," he said as understanding dawned. "You've run into this before, haven't you? No one thinks you can look like that and have a brain, too."

She stared at him belligerently. "What do you mean, 'look like that'? Just how do I look?"

She had the temperament of a hedgehog, but Joe had

to fight the urge to put his arms around her and tell her that he would fight her battles for her from now on. She wouldn't appreciate the gesture, and he wasn't certain why he wanted to make it, since she appeared more than capable of waging her own wars. If he were smart, he would play it safe, make some noncommittal comment to keep from treading on her toes any further, but he hadn't become a fighter pilot because he wanted to play it safe. "Fetching," he replied, and his eyes were hard and bright and hungry.

She blinked, as if startled. She took a step back and said, "Oh," in a soft, befuddled tone.

"You have to know you're attractive," he pointed out.

She blinked again. "Looks shouldn't enter into it. You look like a walking recruiting poster, but it hasn't hurt your career, has it?"

"I'm not defending discrimination," he said. "You asked the question, and I answered it. You look fetching."

"Oh." She was watching him warily now as she sidled past.

He put his hand on her arm, stopping her. The feel of her smooth, warm flesh under his palm tempted him to explore, but he resisted. "If anyone here hassles you, Caroline, come to me."

She darted an alarmed look at his hand on her arm. "Uh—yeah, sure."

"Even if it's a member of your own team. You're civilians, but this is my project. I can have anyone replaced if he causes trouble."

His touch was making her visibly jittery, and he studied her for a long minute, his brows drawing together in a slight frown, before he let her go. "I mean it," he said in a gentler tone. "Come to me if you have any trouble. I know you don't want me to walk you to your quarters, but I'm going in that direction anyway, since I'm turning in, too. I'll give you a thirty-second head start, so we won't be walking together. Is that okay?"

"Thirty seconds isn't very long."

He shrugged. "It'll put about thirty yards between us. Take it or leave it." He checked his watch. "Starting now."

She immediately turned and fled. That was the only word for it. She all but hiked up that tight skirt and ran. Joe's eyebrows climbed in silent question. When the thirty seconds were up, he left the building and caught sight of her slim figure, barely visible in the darkness and still moving at a fast clip. All the way to his own quarters, he pondered on what had turned an Amazon into a skittish filly.

Caroline slammed and locked the door to her Spartan quarters and leaned against the wood as she released her breath in a big whoosh. She felt as if she'd just had a narrow escape from a wild animal. What was the Air Force thinking, letting that man run loose? He should be locked up somewhere in the bowels of the Pentagon, where they could use him for their posters but keep the susceptible women of America safe.

Maybe it was his eyes, as pale blue and piercing as

the lasers she worked on. Maybe it was the way he towered over her, or the graceful power of his muscular body. Maybe it was his deep voice, the particular note in it when he said she was "fetching," or the heat of his lean, callused hand when he'd touched her. Maybe it was all of that, but what had all but panicked her had been the hungry, predatory gleam in those eyes when he'd looked at her.

She'd been doing well up until then. She had definitely been at her off-putting best, both arrogant and dismissive, which had never before failed to keep men at a safe distance. It was a trade-off; it kept her from being friends with her co-workers, but it also stopped any sexual advances before they started. She had battled her way out of so many clinches during college and graduate school and her early days on the job, that she had learned to go on the offensive from the beginning. With all of that experience, she should have been able to keep her composure, but one look from Colonel "Laser-Eye" Mackenzie, one slightly admiring comment, and she had lost both her composure and her common sense. She had been ignominiously routed.

Well, that was what happened when you had Ph.D.s for parents. They had seen the signs of superior intelligence in their only offspring and taken immediate steps to give her the schooling she deserved. All through elementary and high school she had been the youngest in her class, due to her accelerated progress. She hadn't had one date in high school; she had been too weird, too gangly and awkward as she went through puberty two or three years after her classmates.

It hadn't been any better in college. She had started her freshman year right after her sixteenth birthday, and what college man in his right mind would go out with a girl who was legally still jailbait, when there were so many legal lovelies both willing and available?

Isolated and lonely, Caroline had devoted herself to her studies and found herself finishing her senior courses during her eighteenth year. At about the same time the guys in her classes had realized that the Evans girl might be an egghead, but she was easy on the eyes. This time, there was no issue of age to protect her. Having never learned dating skills with anyone her own age, she was totally at a loss on how to handle these...these *octopuses* who suddenly couldn't seem to keep their hands off her. Disconcerted, alarmed, she had withdrawn further into her studies and begun developing a prickly shield for protection.

Her transformation as she reached maturity wasn't drastic enough to equal that of an ugly duckling into a swan; she had simply grown from a gangly adolescent into a woman. Her menses had been late in coming, as if her body had to balance nature by dawdling along while her mind raced ahead. It was all a matter of bad timing. When her classmates were going through puberty, she was still literally playing with dolls. When she went through puberty, they were already settled into the dating game. She never matched them in terms of physical or emotional maturity. When she was ready to begin dating, she found herself being groped by boys accustomed to a much more sophisticated level of intimacy.

In the end, it was just easier to drive them all away.

So here she was, twenty-eight years old, genius IQ, a bona fide specialist in light amplification and optic targeting, possessed of a Ph.D. in physics, reduced to idiocy and panic because a man had said she was "fetching."

It was disgusting.

It was also a bit frightening, because she sensed Colonel Mackenzie hadn't been alienated as she had intended; instead, he'd looked like a man who enjoyed a challenge.

She hit herself on the forehead. How could she have been such an idiot? The colonel was a *jet jockey,* for heaven's sake. He was a member of a different breed, a man who positively thrived on challenge. The way to keep from attracting his attention was to appear meek and mild, with maybe a little simpering thrown in. Problem was, she didn't know how to simper. She should have gone to a finishing school rather than graduate school. She would have taken Simpering 101 over and over until she had it nailed.

Maybe it wasn't too late. Maybe she could act sweet and helpless enough to fool him. No—that would invite attention from the men who *did* like that sort of behavior in a woman. She was caught—damned if she did and damned if she didn't.

The only thing left to do was put up a good fight.

When Joe reached his quarters he stripped out of his uniform, then stood under a cool shower until he began to feel human again. The desert in July was a real bitch, sucking the moisture from his body until even his eyeballs felt dry, but Baby required tight security, and Nellis Air Force Base in Nevada supplied that, in spades. Despite the discomfort and spartan conditions, he was grateful for the security and didn't look forward to taking the wraps off Baby, as would happen when Congress voted on funding. The media would see her then, not that her revolutionary nature was evident in her appearance; her design wasn't radically different from that of the F-22, which was what made it possible for them to do the test flights at Nellis instead of Edwards in California, where test flights were traditionally made. Snoops looked for something different at Edwards, but here at Nellis, with so many different types of aircraft taking part in the war games they conducted, she wasn't so obvious.

The other pilots based here had to notice that they were doing test flights with an aircraft that wasn't exactly like the F-22, but no one who wasn't working on the program was allowed a close look at the Night Wing prototypes, and security was a way of life here anyway. Baby's differences were in her skin and in the electronics suite, her weapons system; when she was unveiled, she would galvanize every hostile espionage agency in the world, and security would have to be even tighter, though he didn't see how it could.

He'd been thinking of Baby, but suddenly the image of Caroline Evans filled his mind and he grinned, wondering what it would take to tame the little hedgehog. His skin suddenly felt hot and tight, despite the cool water, so he shut off the shower and stepped out of the cubicle. It he could get her in the shower with him, they would probably turn the water to steam.

He stood in front of the air conditioner, letting the cold air blow over his wet, naked body and enjoying the shivers that rippled over him, but it didn't do much to ease the sense of fullness in his loins. Grimly he pushed thoughts of Ms. Evans out of his mind. When he was dry enough not to drip, he went, still naked, into the tiny kitchen area and slapped a sandwich together. The freedom from clothes let something inside him relax. He had spent almost half his life in the military, surrounded by regulations and wearing uniforms, and he felt comfortable with it at home, but at the same time there was still a primitive part of him that sometimes said, ''That's enough,'' and he had to strip.

He had grown up on a horse ranch in Wyoming and he returned there every chance he got; spending a week or two riding the roughest broncs on the ranch satisfied the same wild restlessness in him, but he was tied up with the Night Wing project and couldn't get any free time, so the clothes had to go. The only garment he ever regretted having to remove was his flightsuit; if he could just spend all his time in the air, he'd be all right.

Damn it, the higher he was promoted, the less he flew. Responsibilities and paperwork took up more and more of his time. He had accepted the position of project manager on Night Wing only because he'd been guaranteed he would be able to fly the babies. The Air Force had wanted its best in the cockpits of the new planes, and the pilots assigned were all top-notch, but more than that, it had wanted the hands-on opinion of the best of the best, and Colonel Joe Mackenzie still stood head and shoulders above all the others.

Joe wasn't vain about his skill with a fighter, because he'd worked too damn hard to attain it. He'd been born with the intellect, eyesight and lightning-fast reflexes, but the rest was the result of countless hours of study, of practice, of drilling himself in the flight simulator until every reaction was automatic and instantaneous. Even at the age of thirty-five his reaction time was still faster than that of the young Turks coming out of flight school, and his eyesight was still better than twenty-twenty. He had a lot of flying time left, if the military would let him have it. He'd shot up through the ranks so fast that he would probably get his first star in another year, and then he'd be lucky if he could wrangle enough flying time to remain qualified.

The alternative was to resign his commission to take a job with an aircraft manufacturer as a test pilot, throwing away his years in the military. He liked the Air Force, didn't want to leave it, but the idea of being grounded was unbearable. Life would be flat without the challenge of mastering both nature and machine, and knowing his life hung in the balance if he didn't do it right.

Caroline slid into his mind again, a challenge of a different sort plain in her gunslinger's eyes. He could plainly picture the color of those eyes, dark green mostly, mingled with a bit of blue, and gold flecks lighting the depths. The thought of those eyes looking up at him as he moved over her in bed made his heart begin pounding hard and fast, just the way he would take her.

He wanted to make the little hedgehog purr like a kitten.

Chapter 2

Caroline had stringent comfort requirements, which meant it sometimes took her a while to get dressed. If something didn't feel right on a particular day, she took it off and put on something else. Before she left for work each morning she sat, stretched, twisted, moved her arms back and forth, then lifted them over her head to see if her clothes were going to irritate her during the day. She couldn't bear being distracted by an uncomfortable seam or an aggravating fit.

Women's fashions were a sore point with her. Why were most designers men? She thought it should be against the law for a man to design women's clothes. She had decided while still in adolescence that men had no idea how uncomfortable women's fashions usually were and really didn't care, since they themselves weren't called upon to spend hours standing in tendon-shortening high heels, encased in sweltering hosiery, bound either by bras or dresses tight enough to take over the job of lifting and separating, or pushing together to create cleavage, according to the dictates of the occasion.

And why were women's fashions made out of flimsy material, while the temperatures in most offices and restaurants was always set low, so the men in their suits would be comfortable? She found this stupid on two counts: one, why were men required to wear jackets anyway—and was there anything more ridiculous than that remnant of the breastplate, the necktie, that they knotted around their throats like a hangman's noose, interfering with a few basic things like breathing and swallowing—and why weren't women allowed to wear coats, too, if the men felt unable to give theirs up? Fashion, in her mind, consisted of equal parts stupidity and lunacy. In a logical world, people would wear functional clothing, like jeans and loafers and sweatshirts.

She couldn't change the world, but she could control her own small part of it by insisting on her own comfort. Today she chose a full, gathered white skirt that came to midcalf, with an elastic waistband. She topped it with an oversize white T-shirt and twisted two scarves, one melon and one aqua, together to be tied around her waist as a belt. Her shoes were white flats. She was cool, coordinated and comfortable, just the way she wanted to be.

During the night she had tried to analyze just what it was about Colonel Mackenzie that had so discomfited her; other men had come on to her like gangbusters and she'd managed to handle it, so why had his rather mild remark, coupled with a look that wasn't mild at all, sent her into such panic? It was definitely the look that had done it. She'd never seen eyes like those before, pale blue diamonds glittering in a bronzed face, so piercing it felt as if they were cutting right into her flesh, and she'd sensed that the man behind them wasn't like any man she'd met before, either.

There were several possible reasons, but none that she could pin down as the primary cause of her reaction. She would just have to handle herself as well as possible, keep her guard up and try to make certain there were always other people around whenever she had dealings with the colonel. Why couldn't he have come around earlier the day before, when the rest of the team had still been working? If he had, she would have slept better last night.

She glanced around, making certain that everything was switched off, then patted her skirt pockets to assure herself that her keys were in there. Pockets were required; every outfit she wore had to have pockets, because handbags were another of her pet peeves. Why were women condemned to lug them around their entire lives? Why couldn't women have pockets like men? Because fashion said that it ruined the "lines" of their clothes. Because women were thought to be too vain. Because men were continually handing items to women with a casual, "Put this in your purse," meaning, "So you can carry it and I won't have to." For women to be truly liberated, she thought, they should have burned their purses instead of their brassieres. And then thrown their high-heeled shoes onto the bonfire.

To keep from having to carry a bag, she had stocked her desk the day before with the grooming items she was likely to need during any given day. After all, not liking purses was no reason to go without lipstick. She did have personal standards to uphold.

She was normally the first person at work, and that morning was no exception. She liked mornings, and dawn in the desert was something special, with everything so clear and crisply outlined. Later in the day heat waves would blur the edges of the landscape, but right now it was perfect. She hummed as she made coffee. No matter how hot it got, coffee was a necessity in every workplace she'd ever seen.

She tore the wrapper off a honey bun, slapped the pastry into the microwave and zapped it for ten seconds. Breakfast was now ready. She settled into her chair and began rereading a report on the targeting system's last performance as she absently pinched bites from the pastry.

Thirty minutes later Cal Gilchrist came in, looking surprised when he saw her at her desk. "You're in early," he said as he went straight to the coffeepot. "I didn't see you at chow."

"I ate a honey bun here." Having finished reading, she tossed the report aside. Of the other three members of the team, Cal was the most amiable. To be honest, she admitted, he was more amiable than even herself. He was good-natured, friendly and capable, maybe thirty years old, still single and he enjoyed an active social life. She had met him before, but this was the first time they'd worked on a project together. They actually worked for two different companies, she with Boling-Wahl Optics, which had developed the laser targeting system, and Cal with DataTech, which had teamed with Boling-Wahl on the computer program that ran the system.

"There's another test at 0800," Cal said as he sipped his coffee. "When Adrian and Yates get here, we'll all go to the control room so we can listen in on the flights. Colonel Mackenzie's going up today. He always comes back to the control room after a flight, and I'll introduce you to him."

"We've already met," she replied. "He came by last night before I quit for the day."

"What did you think of him?"

She thought for a moment, trying to come up with a concise answer, and finally settled on "Scary."

Cal laughed. "Yeah, I wouldn't want to cross him. I would have sworn that fighter pilots didn't respect anything, but they sure as hell respect him, in the air and on the ground. One of them said that Mackenzie is the best pilot in the Air Force, period. That's saying a lot, considering none of this group are slouches."

The other two members of the team arrived. Yates Korleski, a short, sturdy, balding man, was the senior member and head of the team. Adrian Pendley was Caroline's fly in the ointment on this particular assignment. He was tall and good-looking, divorced, and unrelentingly negative about having Caroline on the team.

When she had first gone to work for Boling-Wahl he had given her the rush, and he'd never forgiven her for the brush-off she had given him in return. He was good at his job, though, so she was determined to work with him, even if it meant ignoring his incessant little gibes.

He walked past her without speaking, but Yates paused beside her desk. "Did you get settled in okay?"

"Yes, thanks. Met the head honcho last night, too."

Yates grinned. "What did you think of him?"

"Like I told Cal, he's a bit scary."

"Just don't ever make a mistake, or you'll find out *how* scary."

"No allowing for human error, huh?"

"Not with his birds or his men."

Yates wandered off in the direction of the coffeepot, and Caroline decided that maybe her panic of the night before had been justified. Yates had been working on defense contracts for twenty years, so if he was impressed, the colonel wasn't any ordinary joe. She grimaced at the inadvertent mental play on words.

At the appointed time they all trooped to the airfield, where the flights were being monitored. Their IDs were checked before they were allowed to enter the control room, reminding her of the tight security. The place swarmed with guards, and she knew that the Night Wing project was only one of several going on. There were a lot of civilians working at Nellis, people with both the highest credentials and the highest security rating. Just being here meant that her background had been checked so thoroughly that her file probably even contained the brand of breakfast cereal she'd liked best as a child.

The control room was a busy place, lined with monitors and people manning them. Practically every part of the Night Wing aircraft incorporated some radical change from how aircraft had been designed in the past, so there were a lot of different companies and defense contractors working to make certain everything was operational. A group of pilots had gathered, too, some in flightsuits and some in regular service uniforms. Several whistles filled the air when they caught sight of Caroline, and one grinning pilot clasped his hands over his heart.

"I'm in love," he announced to the group at large.

"Don't pay any attention to him, ma'am," another of the pilots said. "That's the third time this week, and it's only Tuesday. He's fickle, very fickle."

"But good-looking," the first pilot said in defense of himself. "So what about it, beautiful? Want to get married, live in a rose-covered cottage and have beautiful children?"

"I'm allergic to roses," she said.

"And men," Adrian muttered behind her, just loud enough for her to hear. She ignored him.

"Forget the roses," the pilot said grandly. The tag on his shirt said his name was Major Austin Deale. "I'm adaptable. And fun. Did I mention that we'll have lots of fun?"

A deep voice came over the speaker, and as if a switch had been thrown, the pilots stopped their bantering and turned toward the monitor. It took Caroline a moment to realize that it was an in-cockpit camera, letting them see what the pilot was doing and seeing.

"There are four planes up today," Lieutenant Colonel Eric Picollo said, setting up the situation for them. "Two Night Wings and two F-22s. The F-22 is the only thing in production fast enough to give the prototypes a good test. The Night Wings are doing some stress maneuvers, and then they'll test the targeting system."

The deep voice came from the speakers again, laconic and matter-of-fact, as if the man weren't screaming along faster than the speed of sound high above the desert floor. Caroline shivered, and goose bumps rose on her arms.

"Go to MIL."

"Going to MIL," another voice answered.

"Military power throttle setting," Cal, who was standing just to her right, whispered. "All or more of an engine's rated thrust."

She nodded her understanding, her attention fixed on the monitor. All she could see of Colonel Mackenzie was his gloved hands and long legs, with the throttle between them, but she knew it was him she was watching rather than the other Night Wing pilot. There was just something about the way he moved.

The pilots took the aircraft through a series of maneuvers, and the sensors embedded in the aircraft's skin sent back readings of the stress levels on the airframe.

"Twenty degrees alpha," the deep voice said, confirming what the digital readout on the computer screen was telling them. "Thirty...forty...fifty...sixty."

One of the pilots standing behind her muttered, "Damn," in a nervous tone.

"Alpha is angle of attack," Major Deale whispered, noticing Caroline's puzzled look. His own expression was tense. "Most high-performance aircraft can only do about twenty degrees before they stall out. We've taken Baby to fifty degrees, because her vectored thrust gives better control, but even the X-29 wasn't controllable above seventy degrees."

"Seventy," said the calm voice. "Seventy-five."

The major had turned pale. He was staring at the changing numbers on the computer screen as if he could control them by willpower alone.

"Seventy-seven...seventy-nine...eighty...controls feel a little spongy. That's enough for now, leveling out."

"How'd Mad Cat do?" someone asked.

"Sixty-five," another someone replied, and the group chuckled.

"Was that his alpha, or his pucker factor?"

"I was sweating at fifty."

"We'll have to haul Mad Cat out of the cockpit. He won't have any starch left in his legs at all."

"Bet Breed's heart rate didn't even go up. He bleeds ice water, man, pure ice water."

Next, the aircraft pulled both negative and positive Gs, provoking more comments as the speakers carried the sounds of the grunts the pilots made to force more oxygen into their brains and keep from blacking out. A trained pilot could normally withstand up to six positive Gs before gray-out began, but with specialized breathing techniques tolerance could be raised to about nine Gs for short periods of time.

The colonel was pulling ten Gs.

"Level out, level out," a captain said under his breath.

Major Deale was sweating. "Don't do this to me," he muttered. "Come on, Breed. Don't push it any further."

"Levelling out," a calm voice said over the radio, and she heard the quiet release of air from several pairs of lungs.

"That son of a bitch is a genetic freak," the captain said, shaking his head. "*Nobody* is supposed to be able to tolerate that. How long?"

"Not long," the second lieutenant at the monitor replied. "He actually hit ten for about four-tenths of a second. He's done it before."

"I can only tolerate nine for that long. And he was making sense when he talked! I'm telling you, he's a genetic freak."

"Gawdamighty, think what he must've been like ten years ago."

"About the same as now," Major Deale said.

The next series of tests involved the laser targeting, and Caroline edged her way closer to the monitors. She felt oddly shaky inside, and she tried to gather her thoughts. When she had been chosen to replace Walton on the test site, she had done some quick research on jet aircraft, and that, coupled with her general technical knowledge, told her exactly how dangerous those maneuvers had been. He could have lost control of the aircraft at such extreme angles of attack, or he could have blacked out pulling so many Gs and not regained consciousness in time to keep from drilling the aircraft nose-first into the desert floor. The reactions of the other pilots told their own tale.

Adrian slipped in front of her, effectively blocking her view, since he was so much taller. Caroline brought her mind back to the current situation. She had no doubt he had done it deliberately, and if she let him get away with it he would only do something worse the next time. "Excuse me, Adrian," she said politely. "Since you're so tall, let me stand in front of you so we both can see."

Yates looked up and smiled, either not seeing or choosing to ignore the sour expression on Adrian's face. "Good idea. Step up in front, Caroline."

The targeting test went well. They were currently sighting in on stationary targets, and all of the components performed within the acceptable range. The data streamed across the screen, each item swiftly checked and noted against the hard-copy lists they all carried.

The four aircraft landed safely, and the atmosphere in the control room suddenly lightened to an almost giddy buzz. The laser team stood around Lieutenant Colonel Picollo and went over the rest results with him. Caroline was initially surprised at his knowledge of the subject, then realized that she shouldn't be. After all, he and the other pilots had been working on this project for some time; they would have had to be brain-dead not to absorb some of the information. "The colonel may have more questions,'' he finally said, ''but it looks like we can start testing how well it targets and tracks a moving object now.''

An arm slipped around her waist, and Caroline went rigid. Her head whipped around. Major Deale grinned at her as his arm tightened. Behind him, she could see the other pilots watching and grinning, too. They all looked like posters for a dental convention. Dismay filled her. Damn, it was starting already.

''So, beautiful, where do you want to go for dinner tonight?'' the major asked.

''Hands off, Daffy,'' came a deceptively mild voice behind them. ''Dr. Evans will be with me tonight.''

There was no mistaking the speaker's identity. Even if she hadn't recognized those smooth, deep tones, she would have known by the way her heart began pulsing wildly and her lungs suddenly constricted, making it difficult to breathe.

They all turned around at once. Mackenzie was still in his flightsuit, helmet under his arm. His black hair was drenched with sweat and plastered to his skull, and his eyes were bloodshot from pulling Gs. His expression was calm and remote as he looked at them.

''I saw her first,'' Major Deale protested, but he dropped his arm from around her waist. ''Damn it, Breed, you can't just take one look and decide—''

''Yes I can,'' Mackenzie said, then turned to Picollo and began firing questions at him.

The major turned and gave Caroline a slow, considering look, as if he were really seeing her for the first time, and maybe he was. Until then she had been just a reasonably pretty face, a lark, but now he had to look at her as a person. "I've never seen Breed do that before, and I've known him for fifteen years," he said thoughtfully.

"I don't know him at all," Caroline replied in a tart voice. "I mean, I met him last night. Is he always that autocratic?"

"Breed? Autocratic?" The major pursed his lips.

"Despotic," Caroline elaborated helpfully. "Dictatorial. Peremptory."

"Oh, *that* kind of autocratic. You mean, does he make a habit of commandeering a woman's company for dinner?"

"That narrows it down nicely."

"Nope. First time. He usually has to beat women off with a stick. They love him to death. It's the glamour of his profession, you know, the lure of the wild. Women *looove* uniforms, but underneath he's really dull and boring."

"Daffy..." The calm voice was both patient and warning.

The major looked over Caroline's shoulder and broke into a smile. "I was just singing your praises."

"I heard."

Mackenzie was right at her elbow, but she didn't dare glance at him. She had specifically asked him the night before not to single her out in any way, but the very next time she met him he had all but hung a sign around her neck that said "Mackenzie's Woman." She struggled to subdue the impulse to sink her fist into his belly. For one thing, violence was seldom the answer to anything. For another, he was the project manager, and it would be a very stupid career move. For yet another, he looked like he was made of tempered steel and it would probably break her hand.

So she did the prudent thing and concentrated on Major Deale. "Daffy? As in duck?"

"No," Mackenzie said with grim relish. "As in petunia."

"As in flower child," added the captain, who had been in the group watching the monitors.

"As in...*blooming idiot,*" several others said in unison.

"Petunia," Caroline repeated. "Flowers. Daffy Deale. Daffydeale. *Daffodil!*" she finished with a peal of laughter.

The major gave Mackenzie a dirty look. "I used to have a good, macho nickname. Concise. Thought provoking. Provocative. 'Big.' That's a good nickname, isn't it? Big Deale. It made women think. Was it just a play on my name, or was there a deeper meaning there? Then this...this spoilsport started calling me Daffy, and Petunia, and I got stuck with it."

Mackenzie smiled. Caroline glimpsed it from the corner of her eye, and the reaction she had been trying to ignore was back in full force. She felt simultaneously hot and cold. Shivers ran up her back, but her skin felt flushed.

"Could you see me in my office in half an hour, Dr. Evans?" the colonel asked now. She hated the way he phrased something as a question when the underlying tone made it an order.

She turned and smiled brightly at him. "If you insist, Colonel."

His eyes gleamed with recognition of the way she had forced him to make it an outright order, but he didn't hesitate. "I do."

"Half an hour, then."

As she and the others walked back to their own offices, Adrian paused beside her. "Smart move," he said, his hostility plain. "Snuggle up to the head man and it doesn't matter if you screw up on the job."

She kept her eyes straight ahead. "I don't screw up on the job." There wasn't any point in denying that she had any sort of relationship with Mackenzie, so she didn't waste the effort.

Cal glanced back, saw Adrian walking beside her, and slowed his steps to allow them to come even with him. "The complicated stuff starts with the moving targets, but so far there haven't been many problems with the program. It's almost scary how well the tests have gone."

Adrian walked on ahead without speaking, and Cal whistled softly through his teeth. "He's not the president of your fan club, is he? When we heard you were going to be the replacement he made some snide remarks, but I didn't figure it was open warfare. What's the deal?"

"Personality conflict," Caroline replied. Trying to place the blame was another pointless exercise.

He looked worried. "We have to function well as a team, or Colonel Mackenzie will have us all replaced, and that won't look good on our records. They're under a deadline with these tests. They want something good to show Congress and the media when the vote for funding comes up, and that's in a few weeks, I think."

"I can ignore Adrian," she assured him.

"I hope so. I'll try to be a buffer when I can, but at some point the two of you will have to work together."

"When it comes to work, I think both of us are professional enough to put our differences aside. But thanks for the thought."

Cal nodded, then grinned at her. "So, the good colonel's interested. He made it pretty plain, didn't he?"

"Without reason," she said grimly.

"Maybe from your way of thinking, but not from his."

It was foolish of her, but she began to look forward to meeting Colonel Mackenzie in the privacy of his office. Project manager be damned, she was going to tell him a few things. At the appointed time, she got directions to the appropriate Quonset hut and marched across the tarmac with anger propelling every stride.

The outer desk was occupied by Sergeant Vrska, a burly young man who looked better suited to a pro-football team than a desk, but he greeted Caroline pleasantly and ushered her into the colonel's private office.

Mackenzie had showered and changed into his summer service uniform; the blue of the material only intensified the pale blue of his irises. He leaned back in his chair and watched her calmly, as if waiting for her explosion.

Caroline considered exploding, even though he was

obviously expecting it. For one thing, it would release a great deal of tension. Losing her temper, however, would only give the advantage to him. There was no invitation to take a seat, but she did so anyway, then crossed her legs and leaned back, her manner making it plain that the opening gambit was his.

"I read your file," he said. "Impressive credentials. You were always ahead of your age group in school, began college at sixteen, B.S. degree at eighteen, master's at nineteen, got your doctorate at twenty-one. Boling-Wahl considers you one of the most brilliant physicists in the country, if not the world."

She didn't know what she had expected, but a listing of her accomplishments wasn't it. She gave him a wary look.

"You've never dated," he continued. Alarm shot through her, and she sat up straight, her thoughts darting around as she tried to anticipate where he was going with that line. "Not in high school, which is halfway understandable, considering your age and study load, but not in college or graduate school, either. You've never had a boyfriend, period. In short, Dr. Evans, you don't have any experience at all in handling a rowdy bunch like my men. It upset you when Major Deale put his arm around your waist."

She didn't speak, but continued to watch him.

"We all have to work together, because we have a lot to do and not much time left to do it in. I don't want morale wrecked by hostility, and I don't want you to suffer behavior from my men that makes you uncomfortable. They're men, and they live their lives flying on the edge of disaster. They're wild and arrogant, and they need to blow off steam, typically with booze and women and dumb stunts. One way to keep them from hitting on you is to turn this base into a war zone, with everybody disliking you and not cooperating with you, which won't get the work done. The other way is to let them think you're mine."

She didn't like his phrasing. "That's so Neanderthal, it has hair all over it."

"They won't bother you then," he continued, ignoring her comment. "In fact, they'll be downright protective."

She stood up and began pacing his office. "I just want to be left alone so I can work. Is that such a big thing to ask? Why should I have to hide behind a false relationship?"

"For one thing, they all assume that you've had the normal experiences of a woman your age."

She scowled at him, not liking the way he'd phrased the sentence. Her "age" indeed! He'd made it sound as if she were almost ready to file for Social Security.

"It won't occur to them that their actions could actually be frightening to you," he continued. "There's also the possibility that some of their teasing won't be so lighthearted, that a couple of them might make some serious moves on you and could turn ugly when you slap them down. I can't afford the disruption to the program if I had to bring disciplinary charges against any of my men. I need them, and I need you. Even if they knew you're so inexperienced, it wouldn't keep them from trying to get in your pants. If anything, knowing that you're a virgin would make it worse. The best thing is to mark you out of bounds for them by pretending you're involved with someone else, and the only man on the base they wouldn't consider poaching on is me. So from now on, as far as they're concerned, you're mine. All you have to do is act halfway friendly to me in front of them, rather than glaring at me as if you'd like to have my head on a platter."

"With an apple stuffed in your mouth," she muttered. Then the details of what he'd just said hit her and she stared at him in mortification, her eyes widening and color burning in her cheeks. Damn it, why hadn't she hooted with laughter when he'd talked about her being a virgin? Now it was too late to deny it.

Joe was still watching her with that calm, remote expression, but his eyes were narrowed and strangely intense.

She couldn't meet that penetrating gaze. Her embarrassment was almost unbearable. She summoned her last dregs of composure and said, "All right." Then, for the second time in less than twenty-four hours, she succumbed to the powerful urge to run from him.

Chapter 3

For several minutes after she had literally run from his office, Joe remained leaning back in his chair, his hands clasped behind his head and a small, satisfied smile curving the corners of his firm mouth.

So she was a virgin. He had only been guessing, but it had been a good guess. An experienced woman wouldn't have been so embarrassed or at such total loss about what to say or do. Poor little darling. For all her intelligence, she was a babe in the woods when it came to men and sex, and the reaction she had learned in her youth, when some idiot had probably scared the hell out of her by grabbing at her, had become her standard way of dealing with a man's attention.

He had been in the office before dawn, his mind on her rather than the coming flight and on impulse he had requested her file. It had been interesting reading.

From the time she had started school, she had been separated from her own age group, and she had responded to the inevitable social alienation by devoting herself to her studies, thereby widening the gulf as she outpaced her schoolmates. That wasn't exactly what had been in her file, of course; the impersonal papers had listed only numbers and accomplishments, except for the detailed security check, which had noted the lack of a personal relationship with a man—ever—but neither her psychological profile nor a detailed investigation had revealed any hint of homosexuality. Her work record did reveal a few instances when Dr. Evans hadn't gotten along with a co-worker, always male, but as the field of physics was dominated by men that wasn't in itself meaningful.

Remembering her reaction to him the night before, Joe had begun thinking. Was she so bristly because she had always been the odd man out, socially, emotionally and physically, during her childhood and adolescence? Her own age group would have shunned her, and her classmates wouldn't have been interested in socializing with someone who, compared to them, was a child. By the time she was physically mature and old enough for it not to matter, the pattern was set and she had so many defenses in place that no one could get past all the thorns.

The only way for a man to get close to her was for her to open the gate herself, something that wasn't likely to happen. But then he had seen the way she tensed when Daffy had put his arm around her waist, and the answer had flashed into his mind. A second later he had put his plan into action.

Her work was important to her. For that, she would tolerate the fiction of having a relationship with him, even though she had made it plain the night before that she didn't want to be gossiped about. He knew she was going to be gossiped about under any circumstances, because she just wasn't the type of woman who faded into the woodwork. Given the choice of having to pretend to be involved with him and putting up with the gossip, or possibly not being able to work on the Night Wing project at all, she had chosen the former. He had counted on that very reaction while he had been forming his argument.

Now the other men would leave her alone, giving him an unobstructed field, and he meant to use his advantage to the fullest. She would have to spend time with him, get to know him, learn to relax with him.

Her seduction would be the sweetest mission he'd ever undertaken. Taming that little hedgehog in bed would be more exciting than breaking Mach 3.

Caroline didn't dare return to work; she knew her discomfort would be written plainly on her face for everyone to see, and Adrian would make some snide comments about taking care of her love life on her own time. She darted into the nearest ladies' room and sought privacy in a stall.

She was trembling all over and felt strangely close to tears. She seldom cried, because it didn't accomplish anything except making her nose stuffy. Even more strangely, she had been ignominiously routed again, and it was time she faced the facts.

It wasn't anything Colonel Mackenzie had done that frightened her so; it was her own reactions to him that were terrifying. Intelligence wasn't worth anything if she hid her head in the sand and didn't admit the truth to herself. She had let herself grow too cocky about her ability to keep men at a distance by using her sharp tongue; not only was the colonel not intimidated by it—damn the man, he seemed to enjoy it!—but maybe she had been able to hold off those other men only because she hadn't been attracted to any of them. The shortness of breath, the panic attacks, the pounding of her heart and cowardly behavior, could all mean only one thing: sexual attraction. As an intelligent female, her instinctive impulse was to run for her life.

She excused herself for not having recognized it immediately, because after all, it was the first time she had ever experienced the phenomenon. She hadn't known how to drive a car the first time she had gotten behind the steering wheel, either. She had always been slightly puzzled by both genders' sometimes feverish antics when trying to attract someone of the opposite sex, but now she knew what was at the bottom of it all. Gonads. It was disconcerting to have one's glands turn traitor.

And now there was this situation she had somehow become mired in. She felt certain that if she only applied herself to it, she would be able to come up with some other solution, but her brain didn't seem to want to work. It was probably a side effect of overactive gonads. After all, thinking wasn't conducive to mating.

She tried to organize her thoughts. As the situation stood, she had agreed to pretend to be having a relationship with Colonel Mackenzie so the men would leave her alone and she would be able to work, and also so the men wouldn't be distracted by her. Did the colonel pretend to have a relationship with every woman on base? Why her? What was it about her that was so disruptive that she had to be *neutralized?* She knew she was a reasonably attractive woman, but she certainly wasn't a femme fatale.

And just what would pretending to be involved with him entail? Small talk and smiling? She thought she could handle that. She had never cooed like a lovesick bird the way she had seen some women do, but it couldn't be that difficult. But if he thought this pseudo-relationship involved any hugging and kissing, she would have to call it off immediately, because her heart just couldn't stand the strain. All that adrenaline rushing around couldn't be healthy.

But the situation wasn't unmanageable. If she just kept her head and remembered not to trust him no matter how reasonable he seemed, she should be all right.

With that thought firmly in mind, she squared her shoulders and left her refuge. As she crossed the tarmac, the desert heat scorched the top of her head and made her arms burn. Everything shimmered around her, and her ears were assaulted by the constant roar of jet engines as planes took off and landed. Airmen swarmed everywhere, attending to the business of the huge base. The activity was exhilarating, and even more exciting was the knowledge that she was working on the most advanced jet fighter ever designed.

Work had always been her panacea. She enjoyed it, embraced it, because it was the one part of her life where she excelled, where she fit in. It was comforting and familiar, even though Adrian Pendley was certain to do his best to ruin it for her. Well, if she could ignore Mackenzie, she could easily ignore Adrian.

The colonel's darkly tanned, hawkish face swam before her eyes, forming amid the heat waves, and she stumbled on the edge of the tarmac before quickly regaining her balance. So she wasn't ignoring Mackenzie that well; she would get better at it. For her own sake, she had to.

Sure enough, when she walked back to the office, with her clothing damp with sweat and wisps of hair sticking to her face, Adrian looked at her and sneered. "Didn't you know it's too hot for a quick tussle? You'll learn to save it for a weekend in Vegas."

Yates looked up and frowned. Caroline caught his eye and shrugged to show that it didn't matter.

The laser program was fully developed; they were there as a trouble-shooting team, and since the day's tests had gone well, there was little more to do than recap what they'd seen. Then they went over the next planned test, the first one using a moving target. The aircraft that would be used in the next tests weren't the two that had flown that day, and their targeting systems had already been checked as part of the regularly implemented maintenance schedule. All of that had been done before Caroline's arrival on the base. They did have to check the systems on the aircraft that had flown that day, and she, Yates and Adrian changed into coveralls for the job. Cal remained behind, rechecking the computer data.

"All the different systems people working on the Night Wing project have gotten along well," Yates said as they walked to the hangar. "It's been one of the smoothest operations I've been involved in."

"So don't go screwing it up by insulting any of them," Adrian said.

Yates stopped and swung around to confront Adrian. "That's enough," he said evenly.

"It's only the truth. You know she has a reputation for being hard to work with."

"I know what I'm hearing, and Caroline isn't the one who's being an ass. I hope I don't have to tell you that Colonel Mackenzie can have anyone on this team replaced with one phone call, and he'd do it in a heartbeat if he thought friction between any of us was hindering the work. If that happens, your career at Boling-Wahl would effectively be over, and that goes for both of you."

Caroline stuffed her hands deep in the pockets of her coveralls. Though Yates had been directing his ire toward Adrian, she knew that her position at Boling-Wahl was a bit tenuous, due to her past difficulties on a couple of jobs. One of those incidents had been with Adrian. Perhaps she had been assigned to work with him as a sort of test and her job depended on passing it.

Adrian turned to glare at her. "I'll stay out of her way," he finally muttered, "if she stays out of mine." Then he strode on ahead of them.

Yates sighed, and he and Caroline resumed walking, but at a more leisurely pace. "Ignore him as much as you can," he advised. "I didn't realize the situation between the two of you was so hostile."

"I'm not hostile," Caroline said in surprise.

He gave her a thoughtful look. "No, I don't guess you are. But *he* is. Is it just a case of mutual dislike, or did something happen that I need to know about?"

She shrugged. "I don't suppose it's any big secret. He came on to me when I first started work for Boling-Wahl, and I turned him down."

"Ahh. A hurt ego."

"It would make more sense if we'd been involved and then broken up, but it was never that personal. I guess he doesn't take rejection well."

"That's all it was? You turned him down for a date?" Yates asked skeptically.

"Not exactly. He made a pass at me."

"And you...?"

She stared straight ahead, but she could feel her cheeks heating again. "He was...well, it was a pretty strong pass, if you know what I mean, and I couldn't seem to make him understand that I wasn't interested. I tried being polite, but it wasn't getting through and he wouldn't let me go. So I told him I'd have gone to work at a zoo if I'd wanted to be grabbed by an ape."

Yates chuckled. "Not very tactful, but effective."

That wasn't all she'd told Adrian, but she thought she had admitted to enough. "He took it personally."

"The two of you will have to get along for the duration."

"I understand. I won't snipe back. But if he grabs me again," she warned, "I won't be nice."

Yates patted her arm. "If he grabs you, knock him on the head with something."

She fully intended to.

They spent the rest of the day checking the targeting systems on the two aircraft, and everything looked good. As maintenance crews crawled in, under, over and around the sleek black aircraft, the scene reminded Caroline of Gulliver being swarmed over by the Lilliputians. Lines and hoses snaked everywhere, crisscrossing the hangar floor.

Adrian didn't speak to her except about work, and that suited her fine. He was good at what he did, and as long as he restricted himself to that, she had no problem with him. Maybe Yates' lecture had made an impression on him.

It was late afternoon before they had the two systems thoroughly checked, and Caroline was glad to call it a day. Thoughts of a long, cool shower filled her head. She returned to the office and didn't bother changing out of the coveralls, simply collecting her dress and checking to make certain everything was locked up. Security demanded that nothing be left out on their desks.

When she reached her quarters she turned the air conditioning on high and stood in front of the cold air for a minute, sighing with relief. There was a benefit to having small rooms: they cooled off quickly. She counted herself lucky to have two rooms, period. The first room was a combination living room, dining room and kitchen, meaning that a nondescript couch and matching nondescript chair, with a scratched fake-wood coffee table, occupied one half of the room and the other half was taken up by a galley-size kitchen and a battered Formica table with two chairs. The predominant color seemed to be institutional green. The room was about twelve feet square and opened directly into the bedroom. The bedroom and bath combined were the same size as the front room. She had a bed that was supposed to be double-sized but didn't quite make it, but since she slept alone it didn't matter. There was a scarred chest of drawers, a cramped closet and a cramped bathroom with barely enough room for the essential plumbing, and then only because there was a small shower stall rather than a bathtub. It was livable, but she couldn't see herself ever growing fond of it.

On the bright side, one of the first things she had done had been to replace the light bulbs in the bathroom with new ones of sufficient wattage for the application of makeup. She probably had the brightest bathroom on base. She rather liked the idea.

She took the long, cool shower she had promised herself, gradually turning the hot water off as she became accustomed to the chill, until the spray was satisfyingly cold. She felt herself revive as her overheated skin drank in the moisture. She didn't turn the water off until she was shivering, then dried herself briskly and dressed in loose, cotton knit pants and a big T-shirt, which perfectly suited her notions of comfort.

Now for food. She had decided from the outset to eat in her quarters as much as possible, so she had stocked the tiny kitchen with a few staples. She was standing in front of an open cabinet door studying the contents and trying to decide on her meal when someone knocked on the door.

"Who is it?" she called.

"Mackenzie."

He didn't have to identify himself by name, she thought irritably as she strode to the door and opened it. All he had to do was rumble something in that deep voice.

She braced herself in the opening and felt the heat settle over her like a suffocating blanket. "What do you want?" she demanded. He wasn't wearing a uniform, but the glove-soft jeans, scuffed boots and white T-shirt were oddly disturbing, while the inevitable dark sunglasses every pilot wore hid his eyes. She didn't like it; she didn't want to know what he was like when he was off duty.

Joe noted her challenging stance and the fierceness of her glare. Evidently she had decided that her best course of action was to simply carry on as usual. He was glad; being around her might not be comfortable, but it was sure as hell exciting, and he didn't want that to change.

"Supper," he said.

She crossed her arms. "I'm not feeding you."

"No, I'm feeding you," he said mildly. "Remember? I told Daffy you'd be with me tonight, and everyone will know about it tomorrow if you aren't.'' It was an effort to keep his voice mild and his eyes on her face, because she was obviously braless. The thin T-shirt she was wearing plainly revealed the shape of her high breasts and the darker circles of her nipples. Every muscle in his big body tensed with growing arousal.

''Just a cheeseburger,'' he cajoled in the soft voice he'd often used to calm nervous mares. ''You don't even have to change. Just slip on your shoes and we'll go off base and find a hamburger joint.''

Caroline hesitated. The thought of a cheeseburger was enticing, since she had been about to choose between two brands of cold cereal.

''All right,'' she decided abruptly. ''Give me a minute.'' She dashed into the bedroom and put on a pair of sandals, then raked a comb through her hair. Her freshly washed face stared back at her from the mirror, and she contemplated putting on makeup, then shrugged. A cheeseburger was waiting.

Just before she left the room she remembered that she wasn't wearing a bra and hurriedly put one on. She didn't think he would have noticed, but it was better to play it safe.

He hadn't entered her quarters but was still standing just outside the open door. Caroline turned the lock on the door and stepped out, closed the door firmly, then tried the knob to make certain the lock had caught. Satisfied, she dropped her keys into her pocket.

He was driving a muscular black pickup truck. Caroline looked at him in surprise as he opened the door and she climbed up into the seat. "I never would have figured you for a truck person," she said as he slid his long legs under the steering wheel.

"I grew up on a horse ranch in Wyoming," he said. "I've driven pickups all my life. What did you think I'd drive?"

"Something low and red and flashy."

"I save my speeding for the air." His ice-blue eyes flicked at her. "What do you drive? I know what you're driving now is a rental car, since you flew in, so that doesn't count."

Caroline settled back in the seat. She decided that she rather liked sitting up high so she could see, and she was feeling more comfortable by the minute. Maybe it was the truck that did it; it was such a no-nonsense kind of vehicle. "What do you think I drive?"

"Something safe and dependable."

"Oh."

The one syllable was a little disgruntled. Joe controlled a smile. "Am I wrong?"

"A tad."

"So what *do* you drive?"

She turned her head to the side and stared out the window. "Something low and red and flashy." She had absolutely rebelled against buying anything sedate and conservative. She had wanted power and speed and handling, and had paid a small fortune to get it.

"How flashy?" he asked.

"A Corvette," she said, and suddenly chuckled at the contrast between them.

Joe looked at her again. He couldn't keep from it. She had lived the life of a total egghead, reclusive and socially awkward, but the fire in her couldn't be hidden. It was revealed in the unconscious sex appeal with which she moved and dressed, the fierceness of her temper, the adventurous car she drove. She sat so decorously on the passenger side, but her face was lifted to the hot wind blowing in through the lowered windows. There was a streak of wildness in her that intrigued him, and he shifted restlessly to ease the constriction of his jeans.

They were checked through the gate, and he turned the truck toward the sunset, blazing red and gold in front of them. She didn't seem to feel any need to carry on a conversation; Joe was comfortable with silence, too, so he let it continue.

Caroline couldn't stop herself from glancing at him every few minutes, though she would then jerk her gaze back to the sunset. The T-shirt bared his powerful arms, darkly tanned by the desert sun. He had so many muscles, it was unnerving. She knew that fighter pilots regularly worked out, because a dense muscle mass seemed to help them resist the effects of pulling Gs, but his muscularity was somehow different. He was powerful—the way a panther or a wolf is powerful—from a lifetime of work and using his body. The sun outlined his profile in gold, mercilessly revealing the bladelike bone structure, as clean and fierce as an ancient warrior's face cast on a coin.

She stared at the thin, high-bridged nose, the wide forehead and high, chiseled cheekbones. His mouth was almost brutally clear-cut. The hot wind was sifting through his thick black hair, disarranging the short military cut and her vision blurred as a disturbing vision filled it of this man with his hair long and flying around his broad, bare shoulders. Her heart thumped in a sort of painful panic, and she jerked her gaze away yet again, but it didn't do any good. She could still see him in her mind. It took her only a minute to decide that if out of sight wasn't going to be out of mind, she might as well give in and let her eyes feast.

She turned her head toward him, and her hungry gaze slipped down over his wide, powerful chest to his flat belly. She just couldn't stop it, though neither was she brave enough to let her eyes rest on the fly of his jeans, instead hurriedly skimming on to those long, muscled legs.

She blurted out, "Aren't you almost too big to get into a cockpit?"

He briefly took his eyes off the road to look at her, though the dark lenses kept her from reading his expression. She wished he would take them off. "It's a tight fit," he replied, his voice low and slow and growling. "But I always manage to squeeze in."

The underlying sexuality of his words hit her like a sledgehammer. She was woefully inexperienced but not naive, and there was no mistaking his meaning. Now she was glad he had those dark glasses on, because she didn't *want* to read his expression. She wanted to hide her face in her hands. She wanted to jump out of the truck and run all the way back to the base and the safety of her quarters. Had she been *mad?* She had actually climbed in the truck with this man, and now here they were, alone in the Nevada desert with the sunset rapidly darkening to purple.

Then she remembered that it was her own reaction to him that frightened her, not anything he had done, and she wondered miserably if she should tell him to bail out now while he still could. The way she had been ogling him, he was probably wondering if he would make it back to the base with his pants on, though considering the notorious libido of pilots in general and military pilots in particular, he might not fight very hard. Maybe it was the contrast he presented that got to her the way no man had before, the sense of an intense, smoldering sexuality beneath that cool remoteness. And maybe, if she was lucky, he had no idea of the tumult going on inside her.

Joe was glad of the dark lenses that protected his eyes from the sun, because they allowed him to study her without her being aware of it. She had put on a bra, damn it, but the thin restricting material couldn't quite disguise the pebbled hardness of her nipples. The little darling was aroused—and upset by it; he could feel her tension, see it in the faint trembling of her body that her still posture couldn't control. His eyes went back to her distended nipples, and his hands tightened on the steering wheel as he inevitably began thinking about taking those hard buds into his mouth. She was so beautifully responsive, and she didn't even know it. If she could be so aroused by a naughty comment, what would she be like when he was actually making love to her?

She wasn't the only one who was aroused. If he looked at her nipples one more time, he might have to stop the truck on the side of the road, and she was far from ready for that. To keep himself from making a big mistake, he didn't look at her again until they had reached his favorite drive-in hamburger joint, which was just seedy enough to be interesting.

He parked beside one of the speakers and turned off the ignition, then removed his sunglasses and put them on the dash. "What do you want?"

She wished he had phrased it differently. She leaned down so she could read the menu posted above the speaker and scowled as she forced herself to concentrate on food. The heavenly aroma of frying hamburgers, onions and French fries filled the air; why did the most unhealthy food always smell the best? "A cheeseburger basket and large soft drink."

He punched the button on the speaker, and when a tinny voice answered, he ordered two cheeseburger baskets. Then he half turned toward Caroline, his wide shoulders wedged into the corner of the truck, and casually said, "I'm going to kiss you when we get back to the base."

Caroline stared wide-eyed at him, her heart going into its crazy thumping rhythm again. "I want onions on my cheeseburger. Lots of onions."

"You don't have to be afraid I'm going to grab you," he continued as if she hadn't spoken. "It'll just be a kiss, outside your door where anyone walking by can see us, and someone probably will. I won't even put my arms around you if you don't want me to."

"I don't want you to kiss me," she said, withdrawing to her own corner of the truck and glaring at him across the expanse of the front seat.

"I'm going to anyway. It's expected."

"I don't care what's expected. I agreed to come out with you tonight because it does seem to be a good way to keep all the others in line, but I never agreed to any kissing."

"Don't you like kissing?"

She glared sullenly at him. The perfect answer would be that yes, she liked kissing, but she didn't want to kiss *him.* The perfect answer, however, was a bald-faced lie, and from the way her heart was fluttering like a Victorian maiden's at the prospect of kissing him, she wouldn't be able to carry it off. Lying, she found, seemed to work better when performed with a certain amount of detachment.

On the other hand, the truth was the worst answer she could give him. No, she hadn't liked any of the sloppy kisses that had been forced on her in a hit-or-miss fashion because she'd been fighting like a wildcat to avoid them, but the thought of kissing him made her light-headed, and she was afraid she would like it *too* much.

When she didn't reply he said calmly, "When we get back to your quarters, unlock your door, then turn and hold out your hand to me. I'll take it, lean over and kiss you. It won't be a long kiss, but it can't be a quick peck, either. Does three seconds sound long enough to you? Then I'll let go of your hand and say good-night. On a busy base, any number of people will see us, and the word will spread that we don't seem to be having a flaming affair, but we're definitely involved.''

She cleared her throat. ''Three seconds?'' That didn't sound like very long. Surely she could manage not to disgrace herself for three seconds.

''Just three seconds,'' he reassured her.

Chapter 4

The cheeseburger—without onions—and fries were delicious, reminding her of those few precious times during her childhood when she had been allowed to stay over with her mother's brother and his wife, both of them about ten years younger than her parents, and Uncle Lee had invariably treated her to the biggest, juiciest hamburger she could eat, followed by ice cream, another forbidden food. Her parents had allowed her to eat sorbet or frozen yogurt, but never ice cream. If it hadn't been for Uncle Lee, Caroline thought she might have reached the age of majority without knowing the joys of junk food. She still always felt as if she were having a special treat when she indulged.

After the cheeseburgers, he gave her a slow smile and asked, "Ever played the slots?"

"No. I've never been to a casino."

"That's about to change." He started the truck, and soon they were tooling down Las Vegas Boulevard, an endless array of flashing neon lights in every color of the rainbow. They blinked, they arrowed, they cascaded, they exploded in endless neon showers, inviting one and all to sample whatever it was they were advertising. The big casinos drew the largest crowds, of course, but a goodly number of people were just strolling, tourists determined to see everything in this town geared toward attracting them. People were dressed in clothing that ran the gamut from shorts to formal gowns.

"Do you like to gamble?" she asked.

"I never gamble."

She snorted. "Except with your life. I was in the control room today, remember? Hitting eighty degrees alpha and pulling 10 Gs isn't what I'd call safe living."

"That isn't gambling. Baby was built to give us an unlimited angle of attack, but her capability doesn't do us any good if we don't know how to fly her. My job is to make certain she does what she's supposed to do, get her fully tested out and operational and find out her limitations. I can't do that if I don't exceed what we're already doing in the F-22."

"None of the other pilots are pushing the envelope like that."

His eyes were utterly calm when he looked at her. "They will now. Now that they know Baby will operate under those conditions."

"You did it just to show them it could be done?"

"No. I did it because it's my job."

And because he loved it. The thought echoed in her mind. She had seen it that day when he had entered the control room after his flight, tired and sweaty, his eyes bloodshot, his expression as remote as ever. But his eyes had given him away. They had been fierce and...exalted, the fires of life burning white hot in him.

He parked the truck, and they strolled down the sidewalk. "Do you feel lucky?" he asked.

She shrugged. "How does lucky feel?"

"Want to try it?"

She paused before the entrance to one of the casinos, feeling the cool air gush out through the opened doors. Rows and rows of slot machines stretched before her and even spread out on the sidewalk. Most of them were manned by people automatically feeding in their tokens of worship and pulling the levers. Occasionally there were cries of delight as coins in varying numbers came tumbling out to reward their persistence, but mostly the machines took rather than gave.

"It isn't cost-effective," she said after studying the procedure for a few minutes.

He laughed softly. "That isn't the point. Never gamble if you can't afford to lose, that's rule number one. Rule number two is to have fun."

"They don't look like they're having fun," she said doubtfully.

"That's because they've forgotten rule number two, and maybe even number one. C'mon, I'll stake you."

But she waited another few minutes, until she saw someone abandon a machine that hadn't paid anything in quite a while. The law of averages said it was more likely to pay out than one that had just disgorged a few coins would be to do so again. She sat down in front of it and fed in the quarters, feeling like an idiot as she did so. Joe stood behind her, softly laughing when the mechanical bandit gave her nothing in return. After she had fed in about five dollars without winning anything, Caroline began to take it personally. She muttered warnings and threats as she went through the procedure again—and lost again.

"Remember rule number two," Joe cautioned, amusement in his voice.

She told him what he could do with rule number two, and he chuckled.

She hitched her stool closer to the machine and shoved a quarter into the slot. She pulled the lever and the pictures began whirring, then one by one clicked into place. Bells began ringing and quarters began flooding out of the bottom slot, spilling out onto the floor. Caroline jumped up and stared at the silver coins as other slot players crowded around, offering congratulations, and a smiling casino employee came over. Then she gave Joe a look of consternation. "All those quarters won't fit in my pocket."

He threw back his head and began laughing. She stared at his strong brown throat and felt suddenly dizzy as that damn light-headed feeling swept over her again.

The casino employee, still smiling, said, "We'll be glad to change the coins into bills."

They did, and to her relief Caroline found that the

flood of quarters wasn't a great fortune after all, only a little over seventy dollars. She returned Joe's stake to him and stuffed the remaining bills into her pocket.

"Did you have fun?" he asked as they left the casino.

She thought about it. "I suppose so, but I was beginning to feel a little vindictive toward that machine. I don't think I have the temperament to be a gambler."

"Probably not," he agreed, and took her hand in his to gently pull her out of the path of a man who wasn't looking where he was going. But then he didn't release her as she had expected.

She looked down at their clasped hands. His hand was big and hard, the fingers lean, his palm tough with calluses, but his grip was careful, as if he were very aware of his strength. She had never held hands before, and the touch of palm against palm was surprisingly intimate. She was beginning to realize that fear had kept her from doing a lot of pleasurable things before, but then, she had never before been even tempted to explore them. Her reactions to other men who had tried to venture into a physical relationship with her had varied from bored and disinterested to absolute revulsion.

She could tug her hand free. That was the safest course of action, but somehow she couldn't do it. So she ignored the situation, acted as if her hand wasn't nestled in his much more powerful one like a bird taking shelter, and inwardly she savored every moment of it.

Finally they walked back to the truck, and she realized she was reluctant for the night to come to an end. It was her first date, if she cared to categorize it as such, and it was almost over.

They were both silent on the drive back to the base, and inevitably her mind turned to the coming kiss. She felt both panicked and excited. Another first for her, the first kiss she had actually agreed to and welcomed. It was a toss-up whether she would bolt in fear or hurl herself into his arms.

The moment of truth came all too soon. He parked in front of her quarters and got out to walk around the truck and open the door for her. There were a number of personnel going about their business, glancing at them with idle curiosity, and she knew he had perfectly gauged the situation.

She took out her keys and unlocked the door, then turned and faced him in the colorless glow of the vapor lights overhead. Her eyes were solemn and defenseless as she stared at him, his eyes glittering like ice.

''Hold out your hand,'' he commanded softly, and she obeyed.

His hard, warm hand enclosed her fingers, and he pulled her closer even as he bent. His mouth lightly touched hers, lifted, settled again. He turned his head slightly to adjust the pressure, and somehow the motion parted her own lips, so that they yielded to the molding of his.

His taste was warm and pleasant and...male. The scent of him enveloped her, and she shivered in response. His mouth was still on hers, moving gently. She felt the tip of his tongue touch and tease, making her stiffen at the jumbled memory of some uninvited, intrusive kiss, but this was nothing like that. She felt enticed rather than coerced, and his taste was filling her senses. Warm pleasure shuddered up from her depths; with a little whimper she opened her mouth, and slowly he took her.

The carnality of it was staggering, and so was her reaction to it. She heard herself whimper again, and then somehow she was pressed hard against him, her head tilted up and back to give him deeper access, an access he took with a hard male dominance that stunned her. She felt weak and hot, and her breasts tightened with an ache that contact with his hard chest both soothed and intensified. Her loins felt hot, too, as coils of pleasure tightened deep inside. She was clinging to his hand like a lifeline.

Slowly he lifted his mouth, and it was all he could force himself to do to break the contact. He gave in to the temptation to take several more quick kisses from the soft, innocent mouth that had so quickly warmed to awareness, then he *had* to release her hand and step back. He had promised her. He wanted nothing more than to shove her inside her dark quarters and carry her down to the floor, mounting her with quick, hard urgency, but restraint now would bring him much sweeter rewards in the future. So he controlled his rough, quick breathing and tried to control the fierce rush of blood through his veins.

"Three seconds," he said.

Her eyes were glazed as she stared at him, and she was weaving slightly. "Yes," she whispered. "Three seconds."

She didn't move. He put his hands on her shoulders and turned her around. "Go inside, Caroline." His voice was low and calm. "Good night."

"Good night." She moved jerkily to obey, and as she reached the threshold she paused to look at him over her shoulder. Her eyes were huge and dark with some indefinable emotion. "That was much longer than three seconds."

She switched on the light, then closed and carefully locked the door. Even as she turned the bolt, she heard him drive away, telling her that he hadn't been tempted to linger for even a second, or hadn't considered the idea of knocking on her door. He had accomplished his mission, which was to establish their "relationship," so as far as he was concerned, there was no reason to hang around.

She sat down on the couch and remained there, motionless, for quite some time. She had some thinking to do, and she always concentrated better if she could just sit still and totally lock herself inside her brain, or perhaps it was more a matter of locking everything else *out,* and that included physical stimuli.

It hadn't taken any psychoanalysis for her to understand years ago how her upbringing and accelerated progress through school had combined with her own nature to make her the odd man out, but she hadn't minded. Why should she worry that she had never learned how to associate with the opposite sex on a social and emotional level, when there hadn't been anyone of the opposite sex she was interested in associating with anyway? So she had never regretted her out-of-sync relationship with the rest of the world—until now.

Now, for the first time, she was strongly attracted to a man and wanted him to be attracted to her, but how did she go about accomplishing that feat? When other girls had been learning how, she had been studying physics. She was an expert in laser optics, but she didn't know a damn thing about flirting.

Why couldn't she have gotten her feet wet with someone less challenging, say a fellow physicist who had also spent more time with books than people and was a little awkward socially, too? But, no, instead she had fallen head over heels in *attraction* with a hotshot fighter pilot, a man who could make women go weak in the knees with one look from those diamond-blue eyes. She didn't have to be an expert at kissing to be able to tell that *he* was, and she had a sneaking suspicion that she had made a fool out of herself. All he had done was hold her hand, as he'd promised, and she had practically been all over him. She had a distinct memory of pushing hard against him and rubbing her front against his like a cat, and thinking that she was going to fall in a heap at his feet.

He'd been nice to her this evening. He'd treated her as a friend, had let her relax, and she had had fun. She couldn't remember the last time she had done something so totally useless and enjoyed it. Simple playing hadn't been part of her childhood; her parents had carefully monitored her activities to make certain they were geared toward her educational progress. No ABC blocks for her; she had used flash cards. In defense of her parents, though, she had been an impatient child, irascible when the pace had lagged behind the speed of her inquisitive, hungry intellect. Her childhood hadn't been unhappy, just different, and she had made her own choices in life.

She was groping her way through unfamiliar territory, but Caroline's approach to any problem was to tackle it head-on. She didn't really know how to use the weapons nature had given her, but Joe Mackenzie was about to find them all brought to bear on him.

The first step in solving any problem was to research the subject. It was early enough that a lot of people were still awake, and there were plenty of female Air Force personnel who turned out to be willing to lend her magazines with articles that she thought addressed the problem, and she was even able to come up with quite a bit of research on fighter pilots in general. She was an accomplished speed reader and sat up for several hours plowing her way through magazines offering such intriguing articles as "He's Bad, Bad, Bad— So Why Do You Love Him Anyway?" and "Finding The Gold in The Dross— When Not To Give Up." Double titles seemed to abound, as well as hundreds of glossy photos of women five feet nine inches tall who weighed a hundred and fifteen pounds, most of which was evidently hair and breasts. She learned how to tell when he was cheating, and how to get revenge. She learned how to break into real estate or start her own company, how to win at blackjack—she committed that to memory—and where to stay on vacation in Europe. Interesting stuff. She just might subscribe.

The material on fighter pilots was even more interesting.

She was in the office before dawn, dressed in a loose, lightweight jumpsuit. When she had been making her selection that morning, seduction had collided with comfort, and seduction had lost without even a whimper. The temperature hit a hundred and ten during the day, for heaven's sake.

She hauled out the specs for the day's tests and began rechecking them, making a mental note to ask Cal a few questions about the computer program. She had taken a second major in computer programming, which had seemed to be a good complement to physics, and it had in fact come in very handy on several occasions. She logged onto the computer and began running the tests through it, rechecking once again that everything was as perfect as they could get it.

"How long have you been in—"

She shrieked at the voice right behind her and came up swinging, overturning her chair in the process. Joe's hand shot up and caught her right fist before it could connect with his face, and a split second later he caught the left one in his other hand, the twin movements like lightning.

"Don't do that again!" she yelled, going up on tiptoe to glare at him, thrusting her jaw up to his. Her eyes were still dilated from fright. "What are you trying to do, give me a heart attack? From now on, *whistle* before you get to the door!''

With a deft motion he twisted her arms behind her back, still holding her fists clasped in his palms. The action brought her breasts firmly against him and encased her within his arms. ''I didn't mean to scare you,'' he said softly. ''But if your first reaction is always to attack, you should learn how to do it right, so you won't wind up in the sort of predicament you're in now.'' He saw interest sharpen the dark bluish-green of her eyes and knew that he had successfully deflected her attention from the fact that he was holding her captive.

Caroline considered the situation. She tugged briefly on her arms, but he held her firmly, and there was no way she could free herself from those iron hands. He was too tall for her to hit him in the face with her head. ''I still have the option of stomping your instep and kicking your ankle or knee.''

''Yes, but you're too close to put much power behind it. You can hurt me, but not enough to make me let you go. If I were an attacker, sweetheart, right now you'd be in some serious trouble.''

She wiggled experimentally again, testing her limits of movement. His arms were locked around her, and she was pressed fully against his muscled body. She shivered a little at the unexpected pleasure of it, so surrounded by his warmth and scent. He smelled delicious; she had never noticed any other man smelling the way Joe did, and it wasn't just the fresh scent of soap lingering on his skin. It was a hot, musky scent, subtle and powerful, making her want to bury her nose against him and drink it in. The effects were strong and immediate; her breasts began to tingle and ache as her nipples peaked, and hot tension tightened her loins.

She cleared her throat and tried to take her mind off her body's reaction; they were in the office, for heaven's sake. Just because she had changed her mind about wanting to experience more of this man/woman thing didn't mean she wanted to do it *here.* "Umm...so what should I do when I want to attack?"

"You should learn how to fight first," he replied, and pressed a quick, hard kiss on her mouth as he released her.

Her lips tingled from the kiss, and she licked them. His gaze slid to her mouth and darkened. She tried for nonchalance to hide the fact that she was shaking all over. "So, what do you recommend?" she asked as she set the chair upright and briskly backed out of the computer program, just to give herself something to do. She switched the machine off and faced him with a bright smile. "Martial arts?"

"Dirty street fighting would be better. It teaches you how to win any way you can, and to hell with fighting fair. It's the only way you should ever go into a fight."

"You mean like throwing dirt in the guy's eyes and stuff like that?"

"Whatever works. The idea is to win, and stay alive."

"Is that the way you fight?" she asked. She desperately needed to sit down, her legs were shaking so much, but he would tower over her if she did, and the thought of that made her nervous, too. She compromised by propping herself on the edge of the desk. "Is that what the Air Force teaches its pilots now?"

"No, that's the way I was taught to fight when I was a kid."

"Who taught you?"

"My father."

She supposed it was a masculine bonding thing. Her father had taught her calculus, but that wasn't quite the same.

"I've been researching the typical fighter pilot," she said. "It's interesting reading. In some ways, you're the perfect stereotype."

"Is that so?" He showed his teeth in a very white smile, though maybe it wasn't a smile at all.

"Well, in some ways you're atypical. You're unusually tall, more suited to a bomber than a fighter. But fighter pilots are typically intelligent, aggressive, arrogant and as determined—maybe *stubborn* is a better word—as a bulldog. They want to be in control at all times."

He crossed his arms over his chest, dark lashes shadowing his glittering eyes.

"Fighter pilots have keen eyesight and fast reactions. Most of you have blue or light-colored eyes, so you're certainly typical on that. And here's an interesting little tidbit…fighter pilots usually have more female children than male."

"Finding out will be fun," he drawled.

She cleared her throat. "Actually, I thought you might already know."

He lifted his eyebrows. "Why's that?"

"I *did* notice that they called you Breed. I assumed it's because you do it so well."

One corner of his mouth moved in a slow smile. "My breeding productivity doesn't have anything to do with it. They call me Breed because I'm a half-breed Indian."

Caroline was so startled that she could only stare at him. "A Native American?"

He shrugged. "That's what you can call it if you want, but I've always called myself an Indian. Changing labels doesn't change anything else." His voice was casual, but he was watching her closely.

She studied him just as closely. His skin was certainly dark enough, with a deep bronze hue that she had assumed was a dark tan. His hair was thick and black and straight, those sculpted cheekbones high and prominent, his nose thin and high-bridged, and his mouth was typically clean-cut and sensual. His eyes, however, were an oddity. She frowned and said accusingly, "Then how can you have blue eyes? Blue is a recessive gene. You should have dark eyes."

He had been alert to how she would receive his heritage, but at her reply something in him relaxed. How else would Caroline respond to something but with a demand for more information? She wasn't shocked or repelled, as some people still were by his mixed heritage, or even titillated, as sometimes happened—though he had become accustomed to that because women were often excited by his profession, too. Nope, she honed right in on the genetic question of why he had blue eyes.

"My parents were both half-breeds," he explained. "Genetically I'm still half Indian and half white, but I got the recessive blue-eyed gene from both my parents. I'm one-quarter Comanche, one-quarter Kiowa and half white."

She nodded in satisfaction, the mystery of his eye color having been explained. She pursued the subject with interest. "Do you have any brothers or sisters? What color are their eyes?"

"Three brothers and one sister. Half brothers and sister, to be precise. My mother died when I was a baby. My stepmother is white, and she has blue eyes. So do my three brothers. Dad was wondering if he was ever going to have a black-eyed baby until my sister was born."

She was fascinated by this glimpse of family life. "I'm an only child. I always wanted a brother or sister when I was little," she said, unaware of the faint wistful note in her voice. "Was it fun?"

He chuckled and hooked his foot in the chair, turning it around so he could drop his tall frame into it. Caroline remained propped against the edge of the desk, still effectively pinned there, because he was in the way, but she wasn't paying attention to that any longer.

"I was sixteen when Dad married Mary, so I didn't grow up with them, but it was fun in a different way. I was old enough to appreciate babies, to take care of them. The best times were when I would go home on leave and they would swarm all over me like little monkeys. Dad and Mary always take off for one night alone while I'm there, and I have the kids to myself. They aren't little anymore, but we all still like it."

She tried to imagine this big, dangerous-looking man relaxed and surrounded by kids. Even just talking about them had softened his face. It wasn't until she saw him that way that she realized what a barrier he kept between himself and everyone else, because there was no barrier between him and his family. With them he would relax the iron control that characterized his every move, lose the remoteness that lay over his expression and in his eyes. The relationship he had with his men was different. It was the camaraderie that is established with a group whose members work together and depend on each other for a long time. That wasn't personal, and in a way it *required* him to retain his control. Suddenly she felt cold and a little lost, because she wasn't inside his intimate little circle. She wanted him to relax that guard with her, let her see the inner man and get close to him. With her recent feminine awakening came another insight, one that hurt even more: she wanted him to want her enough to lose that frightening control. It hurt because he didn't, and she knew it. What was frightening was that she knew it wouldn't matter to her unless she was already far more involved emotionally than she had thought.

She became aware that she had been staring silently at him for several long minutes, and he had been just as quietly watching her, one eyebrow slightly quirked as he waited for her to say something. She blushed without knowing why. He came lithely to his feet, stepping forward, so close that his legs were touching hers. "What's on your mind, sweetheart?"

"You," she blurted out. Why was he standing so close? Her pulse was beginning to race again. What was it about him that being close to him put her brain into neutral and her body into overdrive?

"What about me?"

She tried to think of something clever and casual, but she had never learned how to prevaricate or hide her feelings. "I don't know anything about men. I don't know how to act around them or how to attract them."

His expression was wry. "You're doing okay."

What did he mean by that? She was being her usual blunt self, which had always sent men running. This was more difficult than she'd imagined it would be. She found that she was wringing her hands and was vaguely astonished at herself, because she'd never thought she was the hand-wringing type. "Am I? Good. I've never seen anyone I wanted to attract before, so I'm at something of a loss. I know you said we'd just pretend to have a relationship so your men wouldn't bother me, but would it be too much of a bother for you if I wanted to make it more real?"

"Just how 'real' did you have in mind?" he asked, amused.

Again she was at a loss. "Well, how would I know? I just know that I'm attracted to you, and I'd like for you to be attracted to me, but I've never done this before, so you're asking me to play a game without knowing the rules. Would you hand a football to some guy who'd never heard of the game before and say 'Here you go, buddy. Play ball'?"

His eyes danced at the astringency of her tone, but his voice was calm and grave when he replied, "I see your point."

"So?" She spread her hands inquiringly. "What are the rules? That is, if you don't mind playing."

"Oh, I like a little game now and then."

He was drawling again. She gave him an uncertain glance, wondering if he was making fun of her.

He put his hands on her hips and moved her a little farther back on the desk. Caroline grabbed his upper arms, her nails digging into his biceps. No one had ever touched her hips before, except for one eager beaver who had pinched her bottom and gotten shoved over a wastebasket for his effort. The steely muscles under her fingers made her doubt she would be able to shove Joe anywhere.

He moved even closer and somehow used his hard thighs to spread her legs. She looked down in shock. He was between her legs. Her head jerked back up, but before she could say anything he brushed a light, gentle kiss across her mouth. The contrast between that non-threatening kiss and his very threatening position between her legs disoriented her.

He cupped her face with one hand, slowly caressing her cheek, his fingertips moving lightly over the smooth, velvet texture of her skin. His other hand slipped around over her bottom and firmly pulled her forward until he was nestled intimately in the notch of her thighs. Caroline's heart thumped violently, and she lost her breath, as well as her ability to sit upright. Her bones turned liquid and she sank against him, unintentionally deepening the embrace. The hard bulge of his sex throbbed against the soft yielding of her loins, and she felt an answering throbbing begin deep inside her.

He kissed her again, this time with a slowly increasing demand. Helplessly she opened her mouth to the probing of his tongue. His hips moved against her, between her spread thighs, in the same rhythm as his tongue moved in her mouth. The hard bulge in his trousers was even harder, even bigger.

Her senses were swimming, just as they had been the night before. His tongue probed deep into her mouth, stroking her own tongue and demanding a response. His taste was hot and heady, his skin smelling of soap and man. Her breasts were throbbing, and again the only relief seemed to be contact with his hard, muscled chest. It was all almost too much to bear, but the only alternative was to tear herself out of his arms, and she couldn't make herself do that.

She couldn't, but he could. Somehow she found herself being gently freed and set away from him. She swayed, and he steadied her, his hard hands clasping her arms. She stared up at him a little wildly. Damn his control! Why couldn't he feel even a little of the turmoil that enveloped her? He had gotten aroused, no doubt about *that,* but it hadn't affected his control at all, while she was about to go up in flames.

"The rules are simple," he said calmly. "We have to let you get accustomed to touching and being touched, and find out what you like. We'll take it slow, go a little bit further each time. I'll pick you up at seven tonight.''

He kissed her again and left as silently as he had entered the room. Caroline sat on the desk, trying to get control of her heart and lungs, trying to deal with the empty ache of her body. She was in trouble. She was in big trouble. She had started something she couldn't handle, but she wouldn't have called it off even if she thought she could, and she strongly suspected it was beyond her control anyway.

Unless she was very much mistaken, Joe Mackenzie intended to have an affair with her. A full-fledged, get-naked, lovemaking affair. And she was willing; she was going into this with her eyes open, knowing full well that for him it was likely to be only an affair, while it would be much more to her. He would always be in control, the strong core of him always guarded and remote and uninvolved, while she was well on her way to losing her heart.

Chapter 5

The tests went well that day, which was a good thing, because Caroline was in a daze. Adrian made a snide remark to her when they were alone and she confounded him by giving him a vague smile. She was alarmed at her own lack of concentration. That had never been a problem before; her ability to concentrate was so strong that one professor in college had made the comment that she would be able to read during an earthquake, and he hadn't been far off the mark.

She would never have believed that a man could totally disrupt her thought processes, especially since he wasn't paying her any particular attention. He didn't have to, she realized. He had made his intention plain the day before, and he'd been seen kissing her goodnight; as far as everyone on base was concerned, she was Colonel Mackenzie's woman. He was the alpha male, and none of the other men would challenge him for his chosen mate. She was a little appalled at this demonstration of how little things had changed since prehistoric times, even though she had done her part by going along with him. Now there was food for thought. Had she gone along with him because his suggestion had made sense, or because he was the alpha male and she had felt subconsciously compelled to obey him?

Nah. She had never felt compelled, subconsciously or otherwise, to obey anyone. She had gone along with him because he made her heartbeat go crazy, pure and simple, and it was useless to keep looking for extenuating circumstances with which to excuse herself.

When they were back in the office going over the day's test results and preparing for the next day's flights, Cal rolled his chair over to hers. "So, how'd it go on the date with the boss man?"

Despite herself, her hands immediately started trembling and she laid down the paper she had been trying to read. "Very casual, low-key. Why do you ask?"

To her surprise, his friendly eyes were full of concern. "Well, I've never known you to date before, and I guess I just wanted to make sure he wasn't twisting your arm. He *is* the head man on this project, and he has a lot of influence, not just with the base commander and the men here, but all the way to the Pentagon."

She was touched. "And you thought I might feel I had to go out with him to stay on the team?"

"Something like that, yeah."

She patted his hand, smiling. "Thanks, but everything's okay."

"Good. Adrian isn't bothering you too much, is he?"

"I haven't paid any attention to him, so I guess he isn't."

Cal smiled and rolled back to his own desk.

Caroline checked the time. Three and a half hours until seven o'clock. She had always found her work engrossing, but along with her loss of concentration she had evidently become a clock-watcher, too. No one had ever warned her that associating with men was efficiency-destroying.

For almost the first time in her life she stopped work when everyone else did. She hurried to her quarters, turned the air conditioner on high and jumped into the shower. It was only as she was stepping out of the stall that she realized she didn't know where they were going or how she should dress.

She stared at the telephone. She could call him. She didn't know his number, but that wasn't any problem, because the base operator would. It was the sensible thing to do. She was a big believer in being sensible, so she sat down on the bed and placed the call before she talked herself out of her own common sense. He answered on the first ring. "Mackenzie."

God, his voice sounded even deeper on the phone. She took a deep breath. "This is Caroline. Where are we going tonight?" There, that was just right. To the point, no silliness, a simple request for information.

"Wear a skirt," he replied maddeningly, cutting

through her no-nonsense question to the reason behind it. "Something I can get my hands under."

The receiver clicked in her ear, and she stared at it. The damn man had hung up on her! And her heart was racing again. Damn him, damn him, *damn* him. It wasn't fair. She was all but in a panic with anticipation and fear and wanting, and his heartbeat was probably as steady as a rock.

A skirt? After that comment, he was lucky she wasn't running for the hills. There was no way she could get in that truck with him expecting at any moment to feel those hot, callused hands sliding up her thighs. If he'd kept his mouth shut she would probably have worn a skirt because it was cooler, but if she wore one now, she would automatically be giving him permission to put his hand up it, and God knows what else. And it wasn't that she didn't want him to, just that he'd said they would go slow and that didn't sound slow at all to her, and even if it was, she would like to have a little control over the situation. What she would really like was to destroy *his* control, to have him as hot and bothered and on the verge of madness as she was.

She sat down on the bed and took several deep breaths. Maybe nuns had the right idea. Men were obviously detrimental to a woman's mental health.

She put on khaki fatigue pants and a tailored white shirt. That was as close as she was going to get to a skirt...not very close at all.

He knocked on the door at seven o'clock precisely, and when she opened it he burst out laughing. "What have you been thinking?'' he asked, still chuckling. ''That I'm a big bad wolf all set to gobble you up?''

''The thought crossed my mind.''

He watched as she double-checked the appliances in the small quarters, then locked and double-checked the door. She was a cautious woman indeed. He put his hand on her waist as he walked her to the truck. ''You don't have anything to worry about,'' he said soothingly. ''I'm not going to eat you.'' Three seconds ticked by before he murmured, ''Yet.''

He felt her jump. Her peculiar blend of inexperience and sexuality was slowly driving him mad. When he kissed her, she responded with a heat and intensity that brought him to the brink of violence, but at the same time he sensed that she was ready to bolt at any time. She reminded him of nothing so much as a filly when a stallion is brought to her for the first time, nervous and apt to bite or kick, while at the same time her scent was telling the stallion she was more than ready for his mounting and he was going wild trying to accomplish it. Well, he'd calmed many a mare for both riding and servicing, and he knew just how to go about it.

He lifted her into the truck before she could change her mind and went around to the driver's side. The proposition she had put to him that morning had been in his mind all day, as had the blunt, forthright way she had done it. Caroline didn't know how to be flirtatious or sweetly cajoling; she had just laid it on the line, and her ego with it. He had wanted to take her in his arms and hold her, tell her that she needed to learn how to protect herself better than that. She had no defenses and didn't even realize it. Everything about her was straight ahead, no detours or subterfuges. He'd never had a woman ask for him like that before, ask him to teach her about men and sex. He'd been half-aroused all day, silently cursing the constrictions of his uniform.

Now he was in his customary off-duty jeans and boots, but the jeans were even more restrictive. He shifted position uncomfortably, trying to stretch his leg out to give himself more room. Damn it, he either needed to get out of his pants or get rid of his hard-on—preferably both, and in that order.

"Where are we going this time?" she asked, pushing her wind-blown hair out of her face.

"Do you like Mexican?"

Her eyes lit up. "Tacos," she purred. "Enchiladas. Sopapillas."

He laughed. "Got it." As she pushed her hair back once more, he said, "Would you rather I put up the windows and turned on the air conditioning?"

"No, I like it." She paused before admitting, "My 'vette is a convertible."

He was smiling as he returned his attention to the road. Her name should have been Paradox, because she was one conflicting characteristic after another.

They went to his favorite Mexican restaurant in Vegas, where the best enchiladas she'd ever eaten, coupled with a frozen Margarita, relaxed her and made her forget that she was nervous. Joe drank water with his dinner, something she found curious. "I thought pilots were supposed to be hard drinkers," she said.

"Most of us put away our share of pilot juice," he said lazily.

"But not you?"

"Nope. There's a time limit within which you aren't supposed to drink if you're going to be flying the next day, but I think it's too close. I want perfect control of myself and my machine. The laws of physics and aerodynamics aren't very forgiving at Mach 2." He lifted his glass of water in a little toast. "Not only that, I'm a half-breed. I don't drink. Period."

She gave a brief nod as if admitting the wisdom of that. "If it's so dangerous, why do any pilots drink?"

"To wind down. You're so tense for so long, with the adrenaline burning up your veins, that you can't come down from the high. Our lives are on the line every minute up there, even on routine flights. Hell, there's no such thing as a routine flight."

She started to ask a question about Night Wing, but remembered where they were and left it for another time. Security wasn't something she took lightly.

After dinner she said, "What now?" then wished she hadn't. She also wished she hadn't had that Margarita. She saw his point about needing perfect control.

"Now, sweetheart, we play."

When he said play, he meant play. Ten minutes later they were on a miniature golf course.

She hefted the putter experimentally. "I've never done this before."

"Looks like I'm going to be first with you at a lot of things," he replied with that maddening calm of his.

She scowled and lifted the putter like a bat. "Maybe not."

He kissed her even as he relieved her of the putter with a move so fast she saw only a blur. Disgruntled, she thought that if he'd lived in the Old West he would have been a gunfighter.

"Your first lesson," he said, turning her so her back was to him and putting his arms around her. He folded her hands around the handle in the correct manner and showed her how to swing, smooth and level, hitting the ball with carefully restrained power. Strength wasn't a factor in miniature golf; the game required judgment and coordination.

He made a hole in one on the first green. "You've done this before," she accused.

"Among other things."

"New rule. Each innuendo will add a stroke to your score."

"Good. Added strokes means it'll last longer."

She wanted to throw her ball at him and stomp off the green, but instead she shouted with laughter and firmly added another stroke to his score. Rules were rules.

To her surprise, she seemed to have the needed judgment of distance, force and direction, and challenged him even though she had never played before. He was too aggressive by nature to give her the game and set himself to the task of beating her, displaying intense concentration and superb hand-eye coordination. Caroline was just as determined, and the game was largely played in silence, to a tie. He pointed out that it was a draw only because of the penalty stroke she'd added to his score.

"So let's play another," she challenged. "Throw this one out, and the best two out of three wins."

"Deal."

They had to play five more games, because two others ended in draws. He won the first game, she won the second, and the next two were the ties; he finally ended it by winning the fifth game by one stroke.

She was scowling as they turned in their putters, and Joe was reminded of the look on her face the night before, when the slot machine had kept taking her quarters without making a payoff. He had had the idle thought that she was on the verge of dismantling the machine when it had finally paid out. No doubt about it, Caroline made no pretense of being good-natured about losing. She didn't like it. He understood that, because he didn't like it, either.

On the drive back to the base he slowed and pulled off the road, then drove about a quarter of a mile into the desert before stopping. He killed the lights and motor, and the night silence poured in through the open windows.

"Are you ready for another first?"

Caroline tensed. "What kind of first?"

"Parking."

"Thanks, but I had to pass a test on that when I got my driver's license."

He chuckled at the testy comment but sensed the nervousness behind it. "Here are our rules on making out. Number one, I'm not going to make love to you.

Your first time is going to be on a bed, not in the front seat of a truck. Number two, we're going to keep most of our clothes on, because if we don't, your first time *will* be in the front seat of a truck.''

She cleared her throat. ''It sounds pretty frustrating.''

''It is. That's the whole point of parking and making out.'' He laughed and slid out from behind the steering wheel, then scooped her onto his lap. A little more shifting and he was sitting with his back propped against the passenger door, his long legs stretched out on the seat, while she was lying pressed against his right side, half on the seat and half on him, her head on his shoulder with her face tilted up, and he was leisurely kissing her.

If the windows had been up they would have fogged over. His mouth was slow and hot and demanding, making her forget about time. The slow beat of pleasure began to pound in her veins, and her arms wound about his neck.

His palm covered her breast and the shock jolted her, making her tear her mouth from his. He ruthlessly took it again, stifling her instinctive protest, so she could only whimper into his mouth. As the shock faded, she began to whimper from the pleasure of it, and her nipple beaded tightly beneath the layers of cloth.

''Do you like it?'' he murmured. ''Or do you want me to stop?''

She liked it, maybe too much, but she didn't want him to stop. Her breast was tingling and throbbing, the heat from it spreading down to her loins. His strong fingers were slowly kneading, taking care not to hurt her; then he found the turgid nipple and rubbed it through her shirt. She moaned and arched against him.

"Caroline?" he prompted. "Do you want me to stop? Or do you want more?"

"Don't stop," she said, her voice hoarse with strain. "Please, don't stop."

He kissed her reassuringly. "I won't. I'm going to unbutton your shirt and slip my hand inside. All right?"

How was she supposed to stand that when she felt as if she were flying into a thousand pieces right now? But as soon as he said it, she knew that she wanted his hand on her naked breast, that the barriers of cloth between them were too maddening to tolerate. "All right," she whispered, and somehow her hand was busy with the buttons of his shirt as he unfastened hers. She wanted to feel his bare skin as much as she wanted his touch on hers.

His long fingers dipped inside her open shirt and trailed lightly along the edges of her bra, pausing at the front center fastening. "Umm, good," he said, and deftly unfastened the garment. She felt suddenly vulnerable as it loosened; then he slid his hand inside, and all her nerve endings rioted. His palm was hot and rough, the callused skin rasping over her swollen nipples as he rubbed and lightly pinched. She heard herself moan and buried her face against his shoulder to stifle the sound.

He shifted on the seat so he was more on his side and she was lying flatter. She felt like a doll, helpless to prevent him from moving her as he willed. He spread her open shirt wide, exposing her breasts to the bright starlight shining through the windshield. She had seen men do it to women in movies, but still she was unprepared when he bent his head and closed his mouth over her nipple, drawing it in with a curling motion of his tongue. Caroline arched wildly under the lash of a sensation so exquisite and unbearable that her entire body quivered. He controlled her with those incredibly strong hands of his and the pressure of his iron-muscled legs, pressing her down into the seat, and somehow he was on top of her.

Her heart was beating so hard it hurt, and her blood was pounding through her veins. She clung to him, barely able to breathe as her body adjusted to his weight and unyielding hardness. The jarring unfamiliarity of it was matched by a deeper, more primitive sense of rightness. He moved his thighs, spreading her legs and settling himself between them, pushing the hard ridge of his manhood against her soft folds. ''This is how we'll be when we make love,'' he whispered, pressing slow kisses on her neck and collarbone, then moving down to suckle deeply on both her breasts, leaving her nipples tight and wet and painfully sensitive to the night air when he lifted his head. He eased the coolness with the hot pressure of his chest.

His voice was a low, almost soundless rustle in her ear. ''I'll move like this, slow and easy, until we're both ready to climax.'' His hips rocked leisurely, rhythmically pressing his sex against hers. Caroline's whole body lifted into the contact, her slender hips straining and reaching. She wanted to speak, to beg him to do something to ease this unbearable tension inside her, but all she could do was gasp for air and dig her nails into his shoulders in an effort to communicate her need to him.

"Then, when it's time, when we can't stand it any longer, I'll start moving harder and faster, going deeper and deeper into you."

She made a high, wild, pleading sound, spreading her thighs wider and lifting them to clasp his hips. Her ankle banged the steering wheel, a welcome distraction, because the slight pain eased her body's primal attention, but it wasn't enough. She twisted under him, frantic with heat and need and a deep, empty ache.

Joe caught his breath at her wild beauty, fierce and demanding, with only the starlight shining across her face. Her body was hot and tense and untamed, demanding a satisfaction she hadn't yet known, but the lure of which was compelling her ever closer and closer to the edge. He wanted to unfasten her pants and drag them down, then bare his own loins and drive into her, hard and fast, just as he'd told her. He wanted her naked, lying stretched out before him on a bed to cushion her from the force of his thrusts. He wanted to take her with swift, rough lust, plunging into her hot womanhood from behind so her buttocks slapped against his belly with the raw sound of sex. The blood of his ancestors ran hot and thick through his veins, the blood of warriors, uncomplicated, as forceful as the elements. He saw himself taking her with the sun burning down on their naked skin and nothing beneath them but the hard, hot earth. And she was clinging to him, a warrior's woman, as fierce and demanding as he was. He had known she was wild the first time he'd seen her, a wildness that had been stifled and controlled, but it was there, just waiting to break out.

He hadn't intended to go this far, but she was pure flame in his arms, her response immediate and strong. His hardness stretched painfully beneath his jeans, demanding his own release, and grimly he knew it wouldn't take much. But the seat of his truck wasn't the place to take her virginity; it was too cramped, too awkward, too inconvenient, and he had also promised her that he wouldn't make love to her tonight. Caroline needed to know that she could trust him, so he grimly fought for control. It wasn't easy; he was close to climax himself, racked with frustration, but his iron will slowly won out, and he eased himself from the clinging embrace of her arms and legs.

"We have to stop," he said, making his voice even. It took more effort than he liked. "If we don't, you'll lose your cherry right here."

"Yes," she whispered, reaching for him again. She didn't care if her first time was in a pickup truck. Her body burned and ached, and she needed the surcease of his possession.

He caught her hands and firmly held them down. "No. Not here and not now."

She stared at him, her eyes wild with frustration; then anger exploded hotly through her veins. She shoved at him, fighting to sit up in a flurry of tangled arms and legs, and scrambled away from him. "Then why did you let it go that far if you didn't intend to finish it?" she shouted. "You...you *tease!*"

Frustration frayed his own temper. Damn it, did she think it had been easy for him to stop? "Because I got carried away, too!" he snapped.

"Yes, I can tell," she said with a sneer. "It really shows. Your breathing speeded up a little bit there."

Furious, he grabbed her hand and carried it to the front of his jeans, pressing her palm hard against the rigid length of his manhood. "Maybe this feels unaffected to you, but you came damn close to finding out just how involved I am." His voice was guttural with rage, and that made him even angrier, because it was evidence of just how far his control had eroded.

She jerked her hand away, even though the feel of that thick ridge was fascinating. She was too angry to be diverted. "I didn't say no, did I?" she demanded hotly. "Just what was wrong with here and now?"

He ground his teeth together, savagely fighting both his anger and a violent resurgence of sexual need. It had been a mistake to force her hand down on his groin. "*Here* isn't a bed, and *now* isn't enough time. When I get in you, I'm not going to get up for a long time. A cramped quickie isn't what you need or what I want."

She crossed her arms and stared furiously out the windshield.

He was silent, too, as he mastered his temper and his voice, reaching deep down to find the icy control for which he was famous. He was astonished at how quickly she had made him lose his temper, something he couldn't remember doing since childhood. He had been angry, but losing control was something he didn't permit himself to do. It seemed Caroline had an astonishing knack for breaking through to his primitive impulses, and, even more disturbingly, she wasn't even trying. He had always controlled the relationships he had with women, letting them get only as intimate as *he* wanted, ending things when *he* wanted. The first night he had met Caroline he had coolly decided to have an affair with her, but on his terms and his timetable. It was disconcerting to realize she could not only tempt him to break his own rules but could actually make him fight to control himself.

"My quarters are in the BOQ," he finally said evenly. "I can't take you there. It would be just as inappropriate to use your quarters. Tomorrow is Friday, and I'm off duty this weekend. We'll check into a hotel in Vegas and spend the weekend there."

He assumed she was still willing, she thought angrily, and was disgusted with herself because she was. But he'd made it plain that it had to be his way or not at all. He was the man in control.

"All right," she said through clenched teeth.

The drive back to the base was completed in an atmosphere more like that between adversaries rather than two people who had just decided to begin an affair. When they reached her quarters, she opened the door and jumped down without waiting for him.

He left the engine running and caught her just as she reached the door, catching her arm and whirling her around. ''My good-night kiss,'' he reminded her, and hauled her into his arms.

There was no way anyone watching could have mistaken that kiss as polite or friendly or in the getting-to-know-you stage. He held her plastered to him from knees to breast, her head bent back under the pressure of his kiss. His mouth was hot and angry and overwhelming, forcing her to acknowledge his dominance. For a few seconds she tried to push him away; then she yielded abruptly to the penetration of his tongue and pressed herself even closer to his hard frame, accepting his aggression and meeting it with her own.

He released her abruptly and stepped away, his eyes glittering. ''You won't need to pack a nightgown,'' he said.

She stood silently glaring as he walked to the truck and got in. ''I hadn't planned to,'' she muttered as he drove off.

Chapter 6

Caroline couldn't find her ID tag the next morning. She searched the dresser top where she usually put it, the kitchen table, the cabinet tops, under the furniture, in the dirty laundry where she had thrown the clothes she had worn the day before, even the trash cans, but it wasn't to be found. She sat down and tried to think what she had done with the thing, since she knew she had worn it the day before, but she drew a complete blank. Joe had had her so distracted that she might have eaten it for all she knew.

She couldn't get into the buildings without that tag; they were coded and electronically scanned at the entrances, and anyone entering a classified area without the proper ID set off an alarm that had the security police swarming with weapons drawn. She was mortified that she had so carelessly misplaced it. Security was so tight that cards couldn't be duplicated; the lost or damaged one had to be voided out of the computer system, a new one issued with a new code and that information fed into the computers. Also because of the security, a jillion forms had to be filled out in quadruplicate to authorize and verify the change. Probably even the base commander, Major General Tuell, would have to sign off on it.

She had had it the day before; she couldn't have gotten into the buildings without it. She distinctly remembered it snagging on a file folder. The tag had just been clipped on, so could it have been tugged loose without her noticing it? Probably. Joe's kisses had turned her brain into mush, and she hadn't been able to concentrate on anything but seeing him that night.

If the tag was lying somewhere in the office, why hadn't the alarm been set off when she had *left* without the proper identification? Or was the scan positioned so that it only read the tags of those entering the building, on the theory that if no one without identification got in, they didn't have to worry about who got out. It was a logical theory; she had no problem with it. Her problem was how to find out if her tag was in the office.

She considered her options. If she called the security police to have them check, it would mean reports and explanations, the very thing she wanted to avoid. So she called Cal to get him to search the office for her. If he didn't find the tag, she would report it lost and face the hassle.

It took him several rings to answer the phone, and his voice was groggy. "Hullo."

"Cal, this is Caroline. I'm sorry to wake you, but I think I dropped my ID card in the office yesterday, and I need you to look for it before I report that it's gone."

He made a grunting noise. "Wha—?" He sounded bewildered and still half-asleep. "Caroline?"

"Yes, this is Caroline. Are you awake? Did you understand what I said?"

"Yeah. Yeah, I'm awake. I got it." He yawned into the receiver. "Look for your ID card. Lord, Caroline, how'd you misplace something like that?"

"I think I snagged it on a file folder."

"So wear it on a chain around your neck instead of clipping it on."

Since she had roused him from a sound sleep, she allowed him his disgruntled advice. Maybe it was a psychological thing, but she didn't like chains around her neck, even when they were called necklaces. Instead she would make a mental note to add her ID card to the list of things she double-checked.

"How long will it take you to get dressed?" she asked.

"Give me five minutes." He yawned again. "What time is it?"

She looked at the clock. "It's 5:43."

He groaned audibly. "I'm on my way. Actually, I'm trying to focus my eyes. You owe me one. I wouldn't do this for just anybody."

"Thanks," she said fervently.

She met him outside the Quonset building five

minutes later. He was unshaven, his hair rumpled, his eyes bleary, but he was dressed, and his own ID tag was hanging on a chain around his neck. She stood outside while he shuffled through the door, still yawning. He was back in less than three minutes, carrying her tag, which she took with a stream of thank-you's.

"It was under your desk," he said, blinking owlishly at her. "What are you doing going to work this early?"

"I usually do," she said, surprised. She thought everyone knew her habit of going in early and staying late.

He suddenly broke into his normal, easygoing grin. "I'm going to have to revise my opinion of Colonel Mackenzie downward, since he obviously isn't keeping you up late. I'm disappointed in the man."

She lifted her eyebrows in feigned astonishment. "You thought he would let anything interfere with work? Surely you jest."

"Evidently I do. Well, have fun. I'll mosey on back to shower and shave and mainline some coffee. More moving-target tests today. We need to be on our toes, and I'm barely on my feet."

She gave him a quick kiss on his beard-roughened cheek. "Thanks, Cal. It would have taken forever to get it replaced, not to mention all of the reports."

"Anytime, anytime." Then he snickered. "Or you could have called Adrian to look for it."

"I'd rather face the security police."

"That's what I thought." With a wave, he began trudging back to his own quarters, and Caroline firmly clipped the tag in place with a sigh of relief.

* * *

At six-thirty, she was engrossed in running through the tests when a low, melodious whistle caught her attention. She burst out laughing and looked up, and two seconds later Joe silently appeared in the doorway.

"Another first," he observed. "No flying cups, reports or fists."

He was dressed in his flightsuit, though he wasn't in full harness yet. Her heart was suddenly in her throat. None of the other flights or tests had made her nervous, but abruptly she felt stricken, barely able to breathe. She had never *cared* before, and all of a sudden her objectivity was destroyed.

It took a special type of man to be a military aviator, and even more so to qualify as a fighter pilot. The numbers were still overwhelmingly male, though women were now accepted into fighter training. Analysts were finding that the female jet jockey shared some personality characteristics with the male pilots, mostly coolness under pressure and situation awareness, but in other significant ways the female pilots were indubitably different from the males. The men were naturally arrogant and supremely self-confident; it took that kind of man to *be* a fighter pilot, to have the kind of assurance that would not only allow him to climb into a machine and streak through the sky at three times the speed of sound, but to have the bloody confidence that he could master not only the machine but anything that might happen, and live to do it again. Fighter training only reinforced that supreme self-confidence.

She stared at him, seeing not only the cool confidence in his eyes but the actual eagerness to strap on that lethal beauty he called Baby. He enjoyed the speed and power, the risk, the ultimate challenge of it. He had no doubt in his ability to make the aircraft perform as he wanted and bring it safely to earth again. His air of arrogant invincibility was almost godlike in its fierceness.

But for all his skill and superiority, he was a man, a human being. And men could be killed.

"You're going up today," she said, barely able to force the words through her constricted throat. "You didn't tell me."

One eyebrow rose in a faintly quizzical expression. "I'm going up today," he replied mildly. "What about it?"

What was she supposed to tell him, that she was terrified because his chosen occupation was one of the most dangerous in the world? She didn't have the right to impose her fears on him. There was no commitment between them, only an agreement to have an affair, which officially hadn't even begun yet. It wasn't his fault that she was falling in love with him, and even if he returned the sentiment, she wouldn't tell him she was afraid, because she wouldn't risk the possibility of distracting him when he needed to concentrate wholly on his job.

So she swallowed her fear and fought for control. "You're too…um, I think *overwhelming* is the word, in a flightsuit. What do you have on under it?"

The diversion worked. The other eyebrow rose to

join its twin. "T-shirt and shorts. Did you expect me to be stark naked?"

"I didn't know. I'd never thought about it before." She made a shooing motion with her hand. "Go on, get out of here. You destroy my concentration. I couldn't work all day yesterday after what you did, so I'm not letting you near me this morning."

As soon as the words were out of her mouth she realized she should have known better. The light of battle gleamed coolly in his eyes as he walked toward her. She had inadvertently issued a challenge, and his dominant nature compelled him to call her on it.

She was still sitting down, and he leaned over her, bracing his hands on the arms of the chair and capturing her before she could scramble away. He kissed her, slanting his hard mouth over hers and using his tongue with devastating thoroughness. Her toes curled in her shoes; she surrendered without even the pretense of struggle, accepting his intrusion and welcoming it with unguarded eagerness.

He shuddered and instantly straightened, his face hard with lust. "What are you wearing tonight?"

She struggled to gather her senses, so easily scattered by his touch. "I don't know. Does it matter?"

She had never before seen his eyes so blue and intense. "No. You'll be naked five minutes after we check into the hotel."

The image was shattering. Helplessly she closed her eyes, her mouth going dry. When she opened them again, he was gone.

If she affected him even half as much as he affected

her, he wouldn't be able to fly the damn plane. The fear rose nauseatingly in her throat again, surging back at full force. It took all of her willpower to force it away, but she managed it, because she knew that when it came down to it, that cold-blooded control of his would shut out every thought that didn't pertain to flying, the real love of his life. The truth hurt, but she took comfort in it, too, for as unpalatable as it was it would keep him safe, and that was all she asked.

Cal had been making a point of arriving in the mornings before Adrian, but she had disrupted his schedule that morning and was still alone when Adrian came in. He gave her an almost automatic look of dislike, poured a cup of coffee and sat down without speaking. Adrian didn't bother her much, anyway, but that morning she was so on edge that she scarcely even noticed he was there. She sat at her desk, torn between fear and anticipation. Part of her mind persisted in dwelling on the dangers of test flights, while the other part kept sliding away to sensual images of the coming night. She couldn't believe she was actually looking forward to it, but not even the realistic expectation of discomfort, at the least, was enough to quell her fever. She wanted Joe, needed him desperately, with an instinct so primal that the threat of pain was swept aside like a toothpick in a flood.

But first she had to live through the flights today.

"Dreaming about lover boy?" Adrian asked nastily.

She blinked at the interruption. "What? Oh—yes. I was. Sorry. Did you ask me something?"

"Only about your love life. I'm a little surprised,

though. I didn't think it was men you liked, or have you decided to try some variety?"

Inexperience was not the same thing at all as ignorance, and she knew exactly what he was hinting at. She gave him a cold look, suddenly relishing the idea of a good, clean battle, free of entangling emotions. "Did you know I was always so much younger than the boys in my class that I was almost through college before I was mature enough for any of them to notice me?"

The question startled him; the puzzlement showed on his good-looking face. "So?"

"So they came after me hot and heavy, expecting me to know the score, but I didn't know anything at all about men and dating. I'd never been around kids my own age. I'd never been kissed, never been to a prom, never learned the things other girls learned at parties and on double dates. When those guys came on so strong it scared the hell out of me, so I said and did whatever it took to run them off. Are you getting the picture?"

He didn't, not at first. His incomprehension was plain. But then understanding broke through his hostility, and he stared at her in shocked disbelief. "Are you saying you were *afraid* of me?"

"Well, what else could I be?" she flashed. "You were grabbing at me and wouldn't take no for an answer."

"For God's sake, I'm not a rapist!" he snapped.

"How was I supposed to know?" She stood up and shook her fist at him. "If you hadn't been so damn sure of yourself and thought no woman could resist you, you might have noticed that I was scared!"

"You didn't act scared!"

"So I get belligerent when I feel threatened." She was standing over him now, glaring and all but breathing fire. "For your information, Colonel Mackenzie is the first man to notice how uneasy I was, and *he* doesn't attack me like a hungry octopus." No, all he did was make love to her with that infuriating control of his, reducing her to mush while he remained perfectly clearheaded. That, however, wasn't any of Adrian's business. "I'm tired of your snide remarks, do you understand? Put a sock in it, as of right now, or I'll stuff one in for you."

The shock left his face, and he glared back at her with a return of hostility. "Am I supposed to feel guilty because you're a social misfit? You're not the only one with problems, lady. I'd just gone through a god-awful divorce, my wife had dumped me for a weasel who made twice as much money as I did and I needed a little ego building myself. So don't blame me for not noticing your delicate psyche and pandering to it, because you sure as hell didn't notice mine!"

"Then we're even," she charged. "So get off my back!"

"With pleasure!"

She stomped back to her chair and flung herself into it. After glaring at the spec sheet for about thirty seconds she muttered, "I'm sorry about your wife."

"Ex-wife."

"She probably isn't happy."

Adrian leaned back in his chair, scowling at her. "I'm sorry I scared you. I didn't mean to."

It was an effort, but she growled, "That's okay."

He mumbled something and turned to his own work.

She had sought relief and distraction in anger, and it had succeeded while it lasted, but now that the confrontation was over her edginess came creeping back. Still, it looked like the air might have cleared some between Adrian and herself, or at least settled down, so it had been beneficial in that way.

Yates and Cal came trooping in, Cal still looking rumpled and sleepy, but he gave Caroline a grin and a wink. Then they all went over to the control room for the day's flights. The pilots were still there, four of them suited up in full harness, with straps and hoses and oxygen masks, and wearing speed jeans. Joe and Captain Bowie Wade were flying the Night Wings; Daffy Deale and Mad Cat Myrick were flying chase in the F-22s. Joe was totally absorbed in the job at hand, as she had known he would be, and the knot of fear in her throat relaxed some to actually be able to see it.

She tried not to let herself stare at him but the impulse was irresistible. He was a lodestone to her eyes, and she was fascinated by him. It wasn't just his tall, superbly muscled body or the chiseled perfection of his face, but the aura surrounding him. Joe Mackenzie was a warrior—cool, nerveless, lethal in his controlled savagery. The blood of countless generations of warriors ran in his veins; his instincts were those honed in past wars, in numberless bloody battles. The other pilots had some of the same instincts, the same aura, but in him those things had been condensed and purified, meeting in a perfect combination of body, intellect and ability. The others knew it; it was obvious in the way they looked at him, the respect they automatically gave him. It wasn't just that he was a colonel and in charge of the project, though his rank garnered its own respect, but what they gave him as a man and a pilot they would have given him even had they all outranked him. Some men stood out from the crowd, and Joe Mackenzie was one of them. He could never have been a businessman, a lawyer or a doctor. He was what he was, and he had sought the profession that would let him do what he was so perfectly suited to do.

He was a warrior.

He was the man she loved.

Somehow she had lost the ability to breathe, and it didn't matter. She felt dazed, mired in unreality. There couldn't be any more fooling herself. She had admitted her vulnerability to him, but never the immediacy of it. She had warned herself against the danger of *letting* herself fall in love with him, fretted that she *might* be losing her heart, but it had all been an emotional smoke screen to keep her from admitting that it was already too late. She'd had no more control over it than she had over her own body whenever he touched her, which should have been enough warning by itself. Her only excuse for her own blindness was that she'd never been in love before and simply hadn't recognized it.

She couldn't look at him as he and the three other pilots left the control room. If he'd glanced at her, everything that she was feeling would have been plain on her face, and she didn't want him to see it, to maybe think about it at the wrong time. She felt absurdly naked, stripped of all her emotional protection, every nerve ending exposed and agitated by the merest stirring of air.

All four birds lifted off, and technicians crowded the terminals, intently studying the information already pouring back in from the sensors embedded in the skins of the Night Wings.

Within half an hour they were in position over the test site, where drones would provide them with moving targets at which to aim their lasers. Caroline always anticipated trouble, because in her experience no new system worked in practice exactly the way it worked in theory, but the tests had gone well so far, and she was optimistic that there wouldn't be any major problems. That day, however, seemed to prove her right in her anticipation of trouble and wrong in her hope that it would be minor. The targeting systems refused to lock on the drones, though they had done so the day before. Two different aircraft were up there today, however, and a totally disgusted project manager ordered the day's tests scrapped and the birds back to the base for a thorough check of the targeting systems.

Joe didn't lose his temper, but his displeasure was plain when he strode back into the control room, his hair matted with sweat from the helmet.

"The birds are in the hangar," he said with icy control, including Caroline in his ire as part of the laser team. "The same two are going back up Monday morning. You still have most of today to find the problem and fix it.'' He turned and strode off, and Cal whistled softly between his teeth.

Yates sighed. ''Okay, people, let's get into our coveralls and get out to the hangars. We have work to do.''

Caroline was already mentally sorting through the options. Laser targeting wasn't new; just the way they were applying it was. The problem could be the sensors in the pilots' helmets, those in the missile optics, even the switch that activated the targeting. What was disturbing was that it had happened to both aircraft at the same time, possibly indicating a basic problem in manufacturing or even design. She glanced at Cal and saw that he was frowning deeply, for *he* would be thinking that for both aircraft to experience the same difficulty at the same time could indicate trouble with the programming of the on-board computers. They were worrying about the problem from different angles, but both of them had realized the implications.

This had just been a peachy-keen day from the very beginning. If the night with Joe followed the same pattern, she would probably find out she was frigid.

They worked through lunch, running computer analyses of the sensors to try to pinpoint the trouble, but nothing showed up. Everything seemed to be working perfectly. They ran the same tests on the three birds that hadn't had any trouble and compared the results, again coming up with nothing. Everything matched. According to the computer, there was no reason why the lasers shouldn't have locked on to the moving targets.

It was late afternoon, and the heat had built to an

uncomfortable level inside the hangar despite the best efforts of the huge air conditioners, when Cal reran the tests on the firing mechanisms of one of the malfunctioning units, and on one that was working. For whatever reason, maybe just the gremlins that invariably plagued every project, this time the computer showed a break in the electrical current in the trigger mechanisms. They were all aggravated because the problem had turned out to be so relatively simple after they had driven themselves crazy for hours and forgone lunch when it was something that could be repaired in less than an hour.

She was in a wonderful mood for a romantic assignation: tired, hungry, hot and ill-tempered. She made a point of scowling down at the ID tag clipped to her pocket before she left the building and headed for her quarters.

A long, cold shower made her feel better, though she was still scowling as she literally threw some clothes and toiletry items into an overnight bag. If *he* wasn't such a martinet, they wouldn't have felt so driven to solve the problem. She could have eaten lunch. She wouldn't now feel so frazzled and out of sorts. It would serve him right if she refused to go.

The only thing was, she wasn't that big a fool. She wanted to be with him more than she wanted to eat, more than she wanted anything.

It was only six o'clock when the knock came on the door. She was dressed, but her hair was still wet, and she was still hungry. She threw the door open. "We worked through lunch," she charged ominously. "We got finished—" she turned to check the clock "—thirty-five minutes ago. It was *nothing*—just a break in the current in the switches—but it took us forever to find it, because we were hungry and couldn't concentrate."

Joe lounged in the open doorway and surveyed her thoughtfully. "Do you always get ill-tempered when you're hungry?"

"Well, of course. Doesn't everyone?"

"Um, no. Most people don't."

"Oh."

He held out his hand to her. "Come on, then, and I'll feed you."

"My hair isn't dry."

"It'll dry fast enough in this heat. Are you packed?"

She fetched the overnight bag and did her quick, automatic tour to make certain everything was turned off. Joe took the bag from her hand and ushered her out, closing the door behind him. She stood there and stared meaningfully at the doorknob until he sighed and tried to turn it, to show her it was locked. Satisfied, she walked to the truck. He stowed the bag, then lifted her onto the seat. She had chosen to wear a halter-top sundress with a full skirt, deciding that it no longer mattered if he could slide his hand under it, since she had given him permission to do much more than that, but she nearly had heart failure when that warm, hard hand slipped up under the material and squeezed her bare thigh.

All thoughts of food fled her mind. She stared at him, hunger of another sort building, her need revealed in her suddenly darkened eyes and quickened breath. Joe lightly stroked her inner thigh with his fingertips, then forced himself to withdraw his hand. "*Maybe* I'll feed you first," he muttered.

Chapter 7

They could have eaten sawdust for all the attention she paid to their meal. All she remembered afterward was that the restaurant was cool and dim, and the dry wine had a crisp, pleasant bite to it. He sat across from her, big and masculine, and with that dangerous glitter in his blue-diamond eyes. He was thinking about the coming night, too, and his sexual intent was plain for her to see. He meant for her to know what he was thinking; he made his possessiveness obvious in the way he looked at her, his gaze lingering on her breasts, his voice low and deep with the gentling, persuasive note of seduction.

They lingered over the meal, and the waiting abraded her nerves like coarsely woven wool. Her clothing irritated her; her breasts ached. She blurted out, "Why are we waiting?"

He had been leisurely studying her erect nipples thrusting against her bodice, and his gaze slowly lifted to her face, scorching her with blue fire. "For you to settle down and relax," he murmured. "For night to fall, so you can have complete darkness, if it would make you feel more secure."

"I don't care." She stood up, her face as fierce and proud as a Valkyrie, her hair as pale as that of those virgin warriors. "You'll have to find some other way to relax me."

Slowly he stood, too, his face hard with the force of his surging lust. Silence strained between them as he paid the bill and they went back out to the truck. The heat was still almost suffocating, the sun a huge red ball low on the horizon, bathing everything with a crimson glow. His fierce, ancient bloodlines were obvious in the primal light falling across the stark lines of his face, giving the lie to the facade of civilization he wore in the form of a white dress shirt and black slacks. He should have been wearing buckskin pants and moccasins, his torso bare, his thick black hair falling free to those wide, powerful shoulders.

She remembered her terror of the morning, that he could be hurt or killed during a flight, and knew she would try never to tell him.

He checked them in at one of the Hilton hotels and, still silently, they rode the elevator upward, with the bellboy carrying their two small bags.

He had taken a one-bedroom suite, and the bellboy performed his customary routine, carrying the bags into the bedroom, showing them how to operate things they already knew how to operate, busily drawing open the curtains to let in the fierce red light of sundown. Joe pressed a five-dollar bill into his hand, and the bellhop took off.

She was still standing in the bedroom, her feet rooted to the carpet while she very determinedly did not stare at the king-size bed, and she listened to Joe lock and chain the door. He walked into the bedroom and very calmly pulled the curtains again, plunging the room into a gloom relieved only by what light spilled through the open doorway. The very air felt charged with tension. He opened his black leather bag and took out a box of condoms, placing it on the bedside table.

"A whole box?" she asked in a husky voice that didn't sound like her own.

He came to stand behind her and deftly undid her dress. As it loosened and fell off her shoulders he said, "I'll go down to the gift shop and buy some more when we run out."

She was suddenly trembling madly, for she had worn only her panties under the dress. No bra, no slip, no hosiery. As the dress pooled around her ankles she was left standing all but naked in front of him, her breasts tight, her nipples thrusting forward in aching need. He lifted her in his arms, and her shoes were left behind on the floor, caught in the froth of material.

He placed one knee on the bed as he lowered her to the surface, then remained kneeling that way while he swiftly, efficiently stripped her panties down her legs. Until that moment she hadn't realized how desperately she had needed that small scrap of protection, or how exposed and vulnerable she would feel without them. She made an incoherent sound of protest as she tried to sit up, for she was naked while he was still completely dressed, but the glitter in his eyes as he stretched her out on her back made her stop struggling.

Joe paused, taking the time to study her naked form and savor the primal satisfaction of the moment when she finally lay bare before him, her tender body exposed and his for the taking. He could already see the signs of arousal in her, manifested in the way her nipples had flushed darker and tightened into buds, and in the way her slim thighs, instinctively pressed together to guard the exquisitely sensitive flesh between them, quivered and flexed in a subtle message. Pale curls, only a shade or two darker than her hair, decorated her mound; a small, fleeting smile tugged at his mouth for a second as he remembered that he hadn't thought her hair color was natural. According to the evidence of his eyes, it indisputably was her own. Those blond curls were so tempting that suddenly just looking wasn't enough.

He put his hand on her breast, gently kneading, cupping, his rough thumb circling her nipple and making it draw even tighter. She caught her breath, which made her breast swell even more fully into his palm. With the same calm assurance he stroked his other hand down her abdomen to slip it between her legs, pressing his fingers hard against the soft folds of her womanhood. Lightning shimmered through her, lifting her hips from the bed in an automatic seeking of more. If his thumb had felt rough on her nipple, it felt even more so now as it rasped across flesh so sensitive she quivered wildly at the slightest touch.

It was unbearable and she suddenly fought away from him, rising to her knees on the bed, her breasts heaving with the force of her breathing. Joe stood up and began unbuttoning his shirt.

His powerful torso was bared as he stripped out of the garment, his skin bronzed, soft black hair matting his chest in a neat diamond and running in a silky line down the center of his stomach. His own nipples were small, dark and tight. He kicked his shoes off. Lean fingers unbuckled his belt, unzipped his fly, hooked in the waistbands of both trousers and undershorts and pushed them down. His eyes never left her slim, nude body as he bent to remove them. When he straightened, he was as naked as she.

The strength evident in his masculine body was almost frightening. He could overwhelm her without effort if he chose. Iron-hard muscles ridged his flat belly, corded his rib cage and long thighs. His male length rose thick and full from his groin, visibly throbbing with the force of his lust. Despite the responding heat of her own blood, beating through her veins in rhythm with the throbbing in her loins, she began to have serious doubts about the possibility of this. She made a soft, panicked sound.

"Shh, sweetheart," he murmured softly. "Don't be nervous." His hard hands closed gently on her shoulders, and somehow she found herself lying on her back again, and he was lying beside her, the heat of his big body searing and enveloping her as he folded her close to him. His nakedness was overwhelming, the strength of his sexuality no longer masked either by clothing or the boundaries enforced by society. He continued to soothe her with low whispers that might not even have been words, while his hands stroked slow fire over her.

Caroline clung to him, unsure of herself in this dramatically intensified situation. She had thought he had led her into sensual territory before, but now she found that she had only been loitering in the doorway. If it hadn't been for the pleasure, she would have bolted. But the pleasure…ah, it was slow and insidious and mind numbing, gently seducing her into relaxing her tight muscles; then, when her resistance was gone, it abruptly turned into a thundering storm that crashed through her nerves and muscles. Her slender body quivered with it, drawing tight as a bowstring again, but this time from a different cause, and he was too instinctive a male animal not to immediately sense that difference. His hands moved over her with a sure and shattering purpose, no longer to calm, but to intensify her arousal.

His mouth drew her nipples into wet beads of sensual torment, punished by sharp little bites and soothed by his tongue. She writhed sinuously in his arms, her hips lifting and rolling in an ancient rhythm that called to him as surely as a drumbeat. Once again his fingers delved between the soft feminine folds and found her moist and swollen, aching for his touch; her thighs opened unconsciously to give him greater freedom, an opportunity he immediately exploited. He carefully penetrated her with one long finger, and a wild little sound burst from her throat as she surged upward against his hand. He lingered over her, drunk with the scent of her warm, aroused body, the silkiness of her skin. He would have crushed her against him if he could have absorbed her into himself, so violent was the urge to meld their two bodies together.

His probing touch taught him both the height of her excitement and the strength of her virginity, and his stomach muscles tightened with almost unbearable anticipation. He couldn't wait much longer, but he wanted her so hot that she would willingly accept the pain of his penetration in order to take the deeper pleasure of their joining. She was so tight he didn't know if he could stand it, but he would go mad if he didn't thrust himself into her sweet depths.

She was arching nearer and nearer to climax as his sensual torment continued, her head thrashing on the bed in a tangle of blond hair, her hands clutching at him with desperate strength. She moaned and sank her nails into his chest. "Now." Her voice was hoarse. "Now now now *now!*"

He couldn't stand it any longer himself. He spread her thighs wide and mounted her, his hard weight pressing her into the mattress as his rigid length pushed against the soft heat of her intimate flesh and felt it begin to yield beneath the pressure. Then the exquisite feel of nakedness brought him to his senses, and he drew back from her, from the maddening closeness of penetration. He reached for the box on the bedside table, extracting one of the small foil packets and tearing it open with his teeth.

"No," Caroline said fiercely, pushing his hand away. "Not this time, not the first time. I want to feel *you,* only you."

Her passion-dark eyes glared up at him; her slim, heated body called to him with a primitive message. She was wild and pagan, even more the Valkyrie now when she lay naked, her thighs open to accept the male intrusion that would end her maidenhood. She challenged his domination, demanded his body and seed in this most ancient celebration of fertility.

Joe braced himself on his arms above her, his face savage as he brought his hips back to hers. He was experienced sexually where she wasn't, knew the wild risk they were taking, but this one time, this first time he, too, wanted her without anything between them.

Caroline went still at the first blunt probing.

Their eyes met and held. A tiny muscle in his cheek twitched as he increased the pressure. Pain threatened for her, became a reality, but she didn't try to push him away. She wanted this, hungered for his possession with a violence that made the pain as nothing. He didn't take it easy with her. His penetration was inexorable: invading, stretching, forcing her soft sheath to accept and hold his turgid length. She arched wildly, unable to take any more, and by her own action found that she could. He gave a harsh sound of pleasure.

"Yes," he muttered tightly. "That's right, sweetheart, you can take me. Come on. More. Do it again." The exquisite feel of her was mind shattering, like hot silk, tight and wet and incredibly soft.

Driven by some frantic need she did, and suddenly

he was seated in her to the hilt, the solidness of his possession making hot tears spring to her eyes. The stretched, too-full sensation was unbearable, yet she bore it because the only alternative was to stop, and that was impossible. She was impelled by a need too instinctive for caution, too fierce to slow. The hard planes of his chest crushed her breasts; his hands slid under her and gripped her buttocks with bruising force as he lifted her into his thrusts, and sharp pleasure exploded through her. She clung to him, sobbing and gasping and half screaming.

Grinding his teeth, he fought his own climax and rode her hard, intensifying her spasms of release. Gradually she stopped shaking and the frantic tension eased from her muscles, letting her relax in his arms. A soft, almost purring note sounded in her throat. "Joe," she whispered, just his name, and the lazy pleasure in her voice almost sent him over the edge.

"Now," he said gutturally, rising to his knees. It was his turn, and his need was so savage he could barely control it. He hooked his arms under her legs and leaned forward, bracing himself on his hands with her legs forced high and wide, draped over his arms. She was completely vulnerable to him like that, totally unable to limit the depth of his thrusts, and he took full advantage of it. He drove into her hard and deep, his powerful shoulders hunched with the effort as he hammered into her, and the pleasure hit him just as it had her, without warning, slamming into him like a runaway train. He jerked convulsively under the force of it, a harsh cry ripping from his throat. The spasms went on and on, emptying him into the hot depths of the woman beneath him. When it finally did end, he sank heavily onto her, his chest heaving as his tortured lungs fought for air. His heart was thudding frantically in his chest, and he was so weak he couldn't roll away from her. He'd never felt like this even when pulling Gs, and certainly never from having sex.

He dozed. She should have protested his heavy weight, but instead she cradled him close, loving the feel of his big body crushing her into the mattress. She could barely move, barely breathe, and it was heaven. She ached all over, but especially between her legs, where his heavy manhood still nestled within her, yet she was filled with a sense of contentment that permeated every cell of her body and all but negated the discomfort. Her eyes drifted shut. She had wanted it just the way it had been—raw and forceful. The only thing that could have made it better would have been if he had lost that damnable control of his. It had given a little, but still it had held, whereas she had been helpless in the grip of a wild passion that had known no limits.

"Caroline." His mouth settled over hers just as he said her name, and drowsily she realized that she must have slept, because she hadn't felt him move, but now he was braced on his elbows, her head cradled in his palms. Without pause she responded, her mouth opening and molding itself to his.

A little while later he forced himself to stop kissing her and gently disengaged their bodies. She remained limply sprawled on the bed while he went into the bathroom and came out a moment later with a wet washcloth. She thought she should be embarrassed at the intimate way he cleaned her, but it was beyond her. She yawned like a sleepy cat and curled onto her side when he had finished. "Did I bleed?" she asked, her voice holding only an absentminded curiosity.

"Only a little." He caressed her buttocks possessively, filled with fierce satisfaction that she had given herself to him so completely. She hadn't held anything back, hadn't let discomfort or fear of the unknown prevent her from hurling herself headlong into the situation. He'd never been wanted like that before, had never wanted anyone like that before, with no reservations or restraints, no boundaries. Any other woman would have been frightened by the savagery of his possession, but Caroline had reveled in it. He'd never *been* so savage before, had never allowed himself to give in to the fierceness of his sexual needs. His rampant sexuality had always been held under ruthless control, yet now he had not only given in to it, he had done so without protection. He might have made her pregnant with that one irresponsible act.

He should have been furious and disgusted with himself, but somehow he wasn't. The utter pleasure of it had been too strong to allow room for regrets. A dangerous image formed in his mind, a picture of Caroline swollen with his child, and to his surprise he began to be aroused again.

She was asleep. He carried the washcloth back to the bathroom and returned to turn back the covers and tuck her between the cool sheets. She murmured softly;

then, when he slipped in beside her, she cuddled against him, automatically seeking the comfort of his warmth. He cradled her head on his shoulder, his free arm wrapped possessively around her hips to hold her close. He went to sleep almost as easily as she had.

When he awakened later, his acute sense of time told him that he'd been asleep for about two hours. He was achingly aroused, and by the time he had caressed her awake, she was, too. This time he forced himself to use protection, though for the first time he bitterly resented the thin barrier between their complete intimacy. She gasped a little when he entered her, her tender flesh sore from the first time, but again she wouldn't let him be gentle, even if he had wanted to be. There would be time for gentleness later; for now there was only the flood tide of desire, demanding release. They writhed and surged together in the darkness, the only sound the roughness of their breathing and the creaking of the bed beneath them.

They slept again. He awakened three more times during the night and had her. He wondered when the urgency would lessen.

It was after eight the next morning when he opened his eyes to find the bright morning sun trying valiantly to pierce the heavy curtains. The room was dim, the air conditioning quietly humming, the air pleasantly cool. His body ached from the unbridled activities of the night.

Caroline lay curled on her side, facing away from him, and for a moment he admired the delicate line of her spine. How could such a soft, delicately made body have withstood the demands he had made on it?

The bed was a wreck. The covers were all pulled loose and twisted, and mostly on the floor. At some point during the night Caroline had pulled one corner of the bedspread up to hug to her breasts. Even the fitted bottom sheet had come loose. One pillow was stuffed under the headboard. He had a distinct memory of there having been three pillows, but he had no idea where the other two were. He also had a distinct memory of having placed one under her hips during one of their ravenous encounters. He yawned, wondering if she would want to remake the bed before the hotel maids could see it. He didn't see much point in remaking it at all.

He was hungry and gently shook her awake. "What do you want for breakfast, sweetheart? I'll call room service, then we can take a bath while we're waiting."

She opened one eye. "Coffee," she murmured.

"What else?"

She sighed. "Food." The eye closed.

He chuckled. "Can you narrow it down a little?"

She thought about it. "Nothing green," she finally mumbled into the mattress. "I can't eat green in the mornings."

Stunned by the idea, he shuddered with revulsion. Come to think of it, he couldn't eat anything green in the mornings, either.

He ordered pecan waffles and bacon for both of them, with coffee and orange juice. The impersonal voice on the other end of the line informed him that it would be forty-five minutes to an hour before his order arrived, which was fine with him. He hung up the phone and shook Caroline awake again.

"Do you want a shower or a tub bath?"

"Tub. Can't sit down in a shower."

He went into the bathroom and turned on the faucets of the playground-size bathtub. Despite the size of the thing, the water level rose quickly. He returned to the bedroom and lifted Caroline in his arms. Her own arms curled trustingly around his neck. "Are you very sore?" he asked with concern.

"Not *too* sore, if that's what you're asking." She rubbed her cheek against his shoulder. "It's just that I can't walk."

He stepped into the tub with her still in his arms and carefully lowered himself into the warm water, then reclined against the back of the tub with her between his legs, her back to his chest. She sighed with pleasure as the warm water began soaking the stiffness from her legs and easing the discomfort between them.

She would have expected to be embarrassed by the intimacy that had passed between them during the night, as well as uneasy with their nudity, but she didn't feel any of that. She felt bone-deep contentment, a sense of rightness and completion that she'd never before known existed. He was her man, she was his woman; how could she be embarrassed with him?

He bathed her, lathering his hands with the fragrant soap and gently sliding them over the tender parts of her body, which somehow seemed to need more attention than the other parts. By the time he finished she was feeling very warm and so was he, if the fullness of his hard male length was any indication. She returned the favor and bathed him, but the imminent arrival of their food prevented him from doing anything to relieve his arousal.

There were two thick, hooded terry bathrobes hanging on the back of the bathroom door, and they put them on a scant two minutes before the brisk knock on the door heralded room service. Joe signed the order slip while the cart was immobilized and the covers removed from the dishes.

The delicious scent of coffee brought her drifting in from the bedroom. Joe's eyes sharpened with the quick resurgence of lust. Even with her face bare of makeup, her hair tousled and her body wrapped in a thick bathrobe, she was more alluring than every other woman he'd had or even seen. The men she worked with might call her the Beauty Queen because of her fastidious attention to her appearance, but her attraction didn't rely on it.

She attacked the food with unselfconscious appetite, and he thought that even the way she ate made him hard. When she was finished she leaned back with a sigh of contentment and smiled at him, a lazy smile that made his blood sizzle.

"What are we going to do today?"

He lifted his black eyebrow. His pale eyes looked as hard and brilliant as diamonds, and there was fire in their depths. "I don't plan on leaving the suite this entire weekend," he said evenly. "Unless we run out of condoms."

Slowly she stood up. "Maybe room service will deliver," she said in a voice that was suddenly tight with need, and then she was in his arms.

Chapter 8

She drowned in sensuality that weekend. The two rooms of that impersonal hotel suite became very personal, imbued with the aura and memories of their lovemaking. They didn't leave the suite at all, relying on room service for their food, and never dressing in anything except the bathrobes.

As a lover, he more than matched the strength of her passion. Caroline never did anything in halfway measures; she had been fiercely virgin, and now she was just as fierce in the giving of herself. He had never before given free rein to his appetites, but with Caroline he could. He sated himself with her, and yet never felt as if he had had enough. The hunger would roar back, again and again.

He had no inhibitions. He was earthy and powerful, sweeping her along with him, introducing her to more variations, techniques and positions than she could have imagined. Sometimes he was on top and sometimes she was; sometimes he was behind her. Sometimes he used his mouth, and he taught her how to use hers to pleasure him. He made love to her in the bathtub, on the couch, on the floor, wherever they happened to be.

He had a beeper on his belt, but the beeper remained silent and the outside world didn't intrude on them. She had never before been so completely, overwhelmingly involved with another human being, to the exclusion of everything else. She didn't think about work, didn't fret for a book to read. She simply experienced.

By Sunday morning the initial frenzied hunger had been fed and their lovemaking had become more leisurely, bringing with it the patience to linger over both arousal and satisfaction. An hour of sensual play had satisfied them for the moment, and Joe ordered a late breakfast; then they lounged in the parlor with their feet up while they watched television and caught up on the news. Caroline curled against his side, heavy-eyed with contentment.

He lifted a pale strand of her hair and let it drift down, the sunlight catching the gold and making it glitter. "Where are your parents?" he asked absently, paying more attention to the play of light than to his own question.

"Usually, or at this exact moment?" Her voice was just as lazy as his.

"Both."

"Usually they're in North Carolina, where they

teach. Right this moment, they're in Greece on a summer-long cultural tour. They're supposed to come home the middle of September.''

''Were you lonely when you were little?''

''Not that I noticed. I wanted to *learn,*'' she explained. ''I couldn't learn fast enough to keep myself satisfied. I wasn't a comfortable child to be around, I don't think. If I hadn't had them for parents I probably would have been a complete wreck, but they helped me handle the frustration and didn't try to limit what I learned.''

''You were probably a holy terror,'' he said dryly.

''Probably.'' She felt comfortable with it. ''What about you?''

He didn't answer immediately, and a tiny quiver of unease intruded on her massive contentment. He would talk easily about his experiences as a pilot, about work, but he kept his private life very private. He had relaxed his guard a little in telling her that he was a half-breed, and that he had three brothers and one sister, but very little else. He hadn't related any childhood experiences to let the conversation get very close to him. Of course, she reminded herself, she hadn't known him for long at all, actually less than a week. The speed and intensity of their relationship dazed her, made the flow of time seem exaggeratedly long.

''No, I wasn't a holy terror,'' he finally said. She sensed the remoteness in his answer.

''Are any of your brothers or your sister?''

Because she was so close to him, she could feel the subtle relaxation of his muscles. ''Just my sister, and it isn't that she's destructive or bad tempered, just *very* determined to have her own way. She's a little steam-roller."

His deep love for his family was evident in his voice. She snuggled closer to him, hoping to keep him talking. "How old are your brothers and sister? What are their names?"

"Michael is eighteen. He's just gotten out of high school and starts college next month. He's interested in cattle ranching and will probably start his own spread when he gets out of college. Joshua is sixteen, and he's the best-natured of the bunch, but he's a jet freak, just like I was at his age. Damn his hide, though, he wants to be a Navy flier. Zane is thirteen, and he's...intense. Silent and dangerous, like Dad. Then there's Maris. She's eleven going on a hundred. Small for her age, so delicate she looks like a breeze would send her airborne, and a will like iron. We're all good with horses, damn good, but Dad is sheer magic with them, and so is Maris."

"What about your stepmother?" Anything to keep him talking.

He gave a quiet laugh. "Mary. She's even smaller than you are."

She sat up. "I'm not small." Her chin jutted out belligerently.

"You're not exactly tall, either. Not quite average, I'd say. I'm almost a foot taller than you." He pulled her back down against his side, her head nestled in the hollow of his shoulder. "Do you want to know about Mary or not?"

"Go ahead," she grumbled, and he kissed her forehead.

"Mary is warm and open and loving, and when she makes up her mind to do something she's unstoppable. She's a teacher. I wouldn't have made it into the Academy without her tutoring."

"So you didn't mind when she and your father married?"

"Mind?" He gave that quiet laugh again. "I did everything I could to throw them together. Not that it was all that difficult. Dad was like a corralled stallion. He was determined to have her, no matter how many fences he had to kick down or go over."

His ease and earthy understanding of his father's sexual nature made her smile. For her part, she simply couldn't imagine her own parents as intensely sexual beings, probably because they weren't. She was proof that they did have sex, but both of them were low-key and concerned more with intellectual matters than those of a physical nature. Their love life was probably warm and affectionate, rather than the raw, raunchy, intense lovemaking Joe had swept her into.

"What about your dad? What's he like?"

"Tough. Dangerous. And the best father in the world. Even when I was a little kid, I always knew he'd fight to the death for me."

That was an odd way to describe one's parent, but looking at Joe she could easily believe that his father was dangerous. They were probably mirror images of each other.

"That's enough about me," he said abruptly, though

very little of the conversation had actually told her about *him.* She sensed that wariness in him again as the steel door guarding his inner thoughts clanged shut. He lifted her astride his lap and pushed her robe open, closing his hands over her breasts. "I want to find out about you."

She shivered and looked down at her breasts, at his bronze hands covering the soft, pale mounds. "That's no longer virgin territory to you."

"So it isn't." The blue of his eyes grew darker, more intense. He stroked one of his hands down her belly and into the notch of her legs, lightly probing. "This isn't, either, but it's even more exciting now than it was before. I could only imagine what you'd feel like before, but now I know how tight and hot you are, and how you start getting wet as soon as I touch you." He circled her delicate opening with one rough fingertip, using exquisite care. She shuddered as pleasure rushed through her, hot and sharp, tightening her muscles and giving him the dampness he sought as her body immediately began preparing to receive him. He pushed his finger a little way into her, and her body quickened, her breath sighing in and out of her lungs, a fine quivering seizing her.

Joe pushed his own robe open. He was as ready as a stallion, his thin nostrils flaring at the female scent of her. With his hand on her bottom he urged her forward, positioned her, then reached down to hold himself steady as she sank onto him with a soft, wild cry. She enveloped him, and he moved his hand, using it to urge her closer.

"Now I know how soft you are," he whispered, "and how you shiver around me, how all those sweet little muscles try to grab me tight and start milking me when we're...*damn!*" The last word was low and fierce. Caroline scarcely heard it. She began moving on him, hungry for him, desperate for the release already luring her.

His hands bit into her hips almost as if he would stay her movements, and she whimpered, but then with another muttered curse he grasped her buttocks and moved her in a hard, quick rhythm on his invading length. This wasn't one of the leisurely times; it was fast and ruthless and basic. She grabbed at his shoulders for balance as she began convulsing and only a heartbeat later he joined her, his head arching back, veins and tendons cording in his muscular neck.

Recovery took longer than the act itself. She slumped forward to lie in exhausted silence on his chest. He smoothed her hair away from her face with gentle fingers, then held her close to him. "I haven't been taking very good care of you," he said quietly. "That's twice."

She couldn't think of any way he could take any *better* care of her. "What is?" she murmured.

"That I've taken you without protection."

"But I asked you to." She closed her eyes, savoring in both memory and actuality the intimate feel of him. "I wanted to know everything, feel everything, about you."

"The first time, yes. Even then, I should have had

better sense. And there wasn't any excuse for this time."

At the hardness of his tone she sat up and squarely met his gaze. "I'm neither a child nor an idiot, Joe. I know the risk and the consequence, and the responsibility is half mine. I could have said no, but I didn't. The risk isn't that great. One of the benefits of having an inquiring mind is that I'm curious about almost everything, so I read about it. I know all about rhythm and timing, and we're fairly safe. Safe enough that I'm not going to sweat and watch the calendar."

"There's no guarantee on that. All the timing can give us is better than even odds, and I told you, I'm not a gambler."

"Would you mind so very much?" she asked steadily.

"Wouldn't *you?*"

She shook her head. "No." Her voice was quiet and rock solid.

He gave her a piercing look. She waited for him to ask her why, but he didn't. Instead he said, "I want to know if your next period is even a day late."

His tone of command was so obvious that she snapped off a sharp salute and barked, "Yes, sir!" Sometimes he was very much the colonel.

He laughed and swatted her lightly on the bottom as he shifted her off his lap. She stood up and tied the robe around her. "When do we have to leave?"

"I arranged for a late checkout," he said. "By six tonight."

So their remaining time locked in their private little

world could now be counted in a dwindling number of hours. It was amazing how quickly she had grown accustomed to room and maid service, to having him all to herself, to the intoxicating delights of the flesh. Probably this seclusion would wear thin if it stretched out for a week, but she would like to have that week. It wasn't to be, however. Tomorrow they would both be back at work, she on the ground and he in the air. Tomorrow she would have to deal with the fear all over again, because the man she loved was doing something dangerous and she couldn't stop it. It would be obscene to even try. Joe was an eagle; only death or age would ground him. She would gladly endure years of quiet terror, if only they would be granted.

For now, she didn't want to waste even one minute before they were forced to face real life again.

She didn't know what this weekend had meant to him, maybe only a prolonged, intense roll in the hay, sufficient for the pleasure it provided, but for her the man and the weekend had been the catalyst that had unlocked the passion of her nature. She felt…changed inside, somehow, freer, more content. It was as if she had been viewing life through a gray veil and it had been ripped aside, letting her see the true, vibrant colors. She no longer felt set aside and isolated, but part of it all. She was no longer alone, as she had essentially been for most of her life, from the time she had first realized that her brain made her different. In giving herself to him, she had gained rather than lost, because she now had a part of Joe that would never leave her. He had given her memories, experience…ecstasy. Under his earthy tutelage, she had bloomed inside herself, learned the rich depths of her own nature.

Abruptly, despite her own common sense and in full recognition of the difficulties it would involve, she hoped that the timing had been wrong for her and she was carrying his child.

"What?" he asked, black brows lifted, and she realized she had been standing in front of him staring intently at him for God only knew how long.

A slow smile broke across her face, lighting her up like dawn. "I was just thinking," she said seriously, "that a lot more women would enlist if you'd just pose for recruiting posters in the nude."

He looked briefly startled, then gave a roar of laughter as he surged to his feet. He grabbed a fistful of robe and hauled her to him. "Do you mean you'd share me with the women of America?"

"Not in this lifetime."

"Not even if my country needed my services? Where's your patriotism?"

She reached into his open robe and firmly cupped him. "One place it isn't," she replied sweetly, "is here."

He began to fill her palm as he responded to her touch, despite their recent lovemaking. "I'll give you two days to stop that, then I'm calling the police."

"We don't have two days," she pointed out. She looked at the clock. "We only have about eight hours."

"Then damn if I'm going to waste a minute of it," he replied, swiftly lifting her into his arms. He preferred the bed for prolonged lovemaking. As he carried her into the other room she clung tightly, wishing that time could stand still.

It didn't, of course. It couldn't, despite her wishes. It felt strange leaving their intimate cocoon, but by six-thirty they were headed back to the base. She sat silently, trying to brace herself for the abrupt end to the intimacy they had shared for the past two days. She would sleep alone that night and every night, until the weekend came again. Perhaps even then. He hadn't said anything about tomorrow night, much less next weekend.

She glanced at him. It was a subtle difference, but the closer they got to the base he became less her lover and more the colonel. His thoughts were already on Night Wing, on those sleek, deadly, beautiful planes and how they responded to his skilled hands. Maybe the change in him was that he became their lover rather than hers. They flew for him; they carried him higher and faster than she ever could. She only hoped they would protect him as fiercely, and bring him back to her.

Long before she was ready, he was depositing her at her door. He stood in front of her, those clear, bottomless eyes lingering over every detail of her appearance. "I'm not going to kiss you good-night," he said. "I won't want to stop. I'm too used to having you."

"Then...good night." She started to hold out her hand, then quickly pulled it back. She couldn't share even a handshake with him. It was too much after the concentrated intimacy of the weekend, too much of a temptation, too sharp a reminder that tonight they would sleep alone.

"Good night." He turned abruptly and strode to his truck. Caroline quickly unlocked the door and stepped inside, not wanting to see him drive away. The tiny quarters, luxurious as they were in comparison with most of the temporary quarters on base, were both desolate and suffocating. She quickly turned the air conditioner on high, but nothing could ease the emptiness. Nothing, that is, except Joe.

She didn't sleep well that night. She kept reaching for him, searching for his warmth, for the big, hard, masculine body she had slept draped over and entangled with for the past two nights. Her own body, abruptly deprived of the sensual orgy it had become accustomed to, ached with frustration.

She was awake well before dawn and finally gave up on sleep. Work had always been a panacea for her, so perhaps it would be again. She *was* assigned to the project to work, after all, not to moon over the project manager.

It did help. She managed to lose herself quite satisfactorily in preparation for the day's tests. Joe didn't stop by, for which she was oddly grateful. She was just now getting her bearings back; if he'd kissed her, she would have been lost again. She would probably also have been stretched out across one of the desks with her legs wrapped around his waist. Typically, he had seen the temptation and resisted it. She wasn't certain she could have.

As usual, Cal was the second to arrive. "Where were you this weekend?" he asked casually. "I tried to call a couple of times to see if you wanted to catch a movie."

"In Vegas," she replied. "I stayed there."

"Wish I'd thought of that. It's a fun town, isn't it? Did you hit the casinos?"

"I'm not much of a gambler. Miniature golf is more my game."

He laughed as he got himself a cup of coffee. "You'd better watch living in the fast lane like that," he advised. "Too much excitement can make you old."

If that were the case, she would have aged at least a hundred years over the weekend. Instead, she felt more alive than she ever had before.

Joe wasn't in the control room when the laser team arrived; the pilots were already in the aircraft, engines screaming. The assignments were the same as they had been on Friday: Joe and Bowie Wade in the Night Wings, Daffy Deale and Mad Cat Myrick in the F-22s. All the project teams gathered around their assigned monitors so they could scan the sensor readouts during the flight.

The birds lifted off.

It went smoothly at first, with the lasers locking on to the drones just the way they were supposed to do. Caroline let out a long sigh of relief. She wasn't naive enough to think there wouldn't be any more problems, but at least that particular one seemed to have been solved. They ran through it time after time, at different speeds and ranges. Yates was smiling.

On their return to base, Mad Cat was on Joe's wing and Daffy was shadowing Bowie Wade, to provide visual verification during the flights. Caroline was still idly watching the monitor when suddenly Bowie's target signal lit up. "Did he hit the switch?" she asked aloud.

Yates and Adrian turned back to the monitor, their brows knit with puzzlement. Cal looked up from his own computer. Almost simultaneously, the computer started flashing the red firing signal and all hell broke loose on the radio and in the control room.

"I'm hit, I'm hit!" Daffy screamed, and Bowie was yelling, "This goddamn thing just went off! What the hell happened?"

"What's the damage?" It was Joe's voice, deep and cool, the authority in it overriding everything else.

"No control, my hydraulics are shot to hell. I can't hold it." Daffy's voice was tight.

"Eject!" Bowie was yelling. "Stop screwing around, Daffy. You can't make it!"

The voices were stepping all over each other, and the control room was in an uproar. The pilots there were turned to stone, their faces frozen masks as they waited to see if one of their own made it back or was going to die right in front of them.

Then Joe's voice again, roaring. "Eject—eject—*eject! Now!*"

The iron authority got through to Daffy as nothing

else could have, and the computers registered a pilot ejection.

"I see a chute!" It was Mad Cat. "He's too low, he's too low—"

Then the radio exploded with noise as the F-22 augered into the desert floor.

Chapter 9

Joe was in a rage when he strode into the control room, but his rage was cold, ice-cold. His eyes were blue frost as he fastened them on the laser team. "What the *hell* happened?" he snapped. "The laser cannon isn't even supposed to be activated, much less go off by itself."

They were all at a loss. The systems had checked out perfectly on Friday afternoon.

"Well?" The single word was as sharp as the crack of a rifle. "I nearly lost a man because of it. An eighty-million-dollar aircraft is in tiny pieces all over a square mile of desert. Do any of you have any idea *what the hell you're doing?*"

The control room was dead silent as everyone waited for a reply, any reply. Yates said softly, "We don't know what happened. But we'll find out."

"You're damn right you will. I want a report on this within thirty-six hours, your analysis of the problem and what you've done to fix it. All flights are scrubbed until I know what happened and I'm satisfied it won't happen again." He didn't even glance at Caroline as he turned and walked out, still as furious as he had been when he had entered the room.

Someone whistled softly through their teeth. Yates' face was drawn. "We don't sleep until we know," he said simply.

The loss of the aircraft was bad enough, but it was Daffy's close call that had stretched Joe's control perilously close to the snapping point. Daffy was lost to him anyway: he'd been too low when he ejected for his chute to adequately deploy, and he had landed too hard and too fast. He was hospitalized now with a concussion and a broken left leg.

Bowie, badly shaken, swore he hadn't touched either the lock-on switch or the trigger, and Joe believed him. Bowie was too good, too careful, but the damn laser cannon had somehow locked on and fired by itself, and Daffy had nearly died. The computers would tell them exactly what had happened, but what Joe wanted to know was *why.* The lasers weren't supposed to be activated yet, but the one on Bowie's bird, at least, had been. Had peak energy been used, the F-22 would have been destroyed in the air and Daffy wouldn't have had any chance at all.

Joe's anger was intensified because the misfire was probably linked to the lock-on problem they'd had the

Friday before. Caroline had said the problem was a simple break in the electrical signal and that it had been corrected, but obviously the trouble was much worse than that, and, far from being corrected, it had nearly killed a man. His fury included Caroline; she was part of the laser team, and his relationship with her had nothing to do with her responsibility as a team member. It wouldn't win her any special favors or leniency.

The laser team wouldn't be the only one working late. The loss of an F-22 and the injury of a pilot weren't things the Air Force took lightly. He had to make a report to the base commander and to General Ramey in the Pentagon. Moreover, they couldn't afford this kind of trouble with the Night Wings, not with the vote for funding coming up shortly in Congress. He had to get the tests completed and the kinks worked out; one of the major pluses the project had going for it was that it was coming in on time and under budget, and delays meant money. If the Night Wings were over budget and not working properly when the vote was taken, the project would be in trouble. Funding depended on how well he did his job and demonstrated both the feasibility and dependability of the birds.

His call on a secure line to General Ramey only underlined his concern. "You have to find out what happened with that laser cannon and make damn sure it never happens again," the general said quietly, but those who knew Ramey knew that he meant what he said. "The vote is close, too close for us to afford this kind of snafu. What good is it to have the first feasible

X-ray laser cannon if it's uncontrollable? We have to have it, Joe. The Night Wing project is too important."

"Yes, sir," Joe replied. Having flown the birds, he knew exactly how important they were. An aviator going up in a superior aircraft had a much better chance, all other things being equal, of coming back alive. The Night Wing birds gave a huge advantage to American pilots, and to Joe that meant American lives saved as well as wars won. He had already been in two wars and he was only thirty-five, and the world situation was even more volatile now than it had been when he had entered the Academy back during the Cold War. Brushfire wars sprang up overnight, and all of them had the potential of dragging the rest of the world into the maw, while technology was exploding. Within five years the F-22s would merely be equal to other countries' fighters, rather than vastly superior. The Night Wings would get that edge back—in a big way.

"Is there any indication of sabotage?" the general asked.

"There haven't been any alarms triggered, but I've asked the security police for an analysis of the work patterns to see if there's anything suspicious."

"What's your gut feeling?" General Ramey had the utmost respect for Joe's instincts.

Joe paused. "A catastrophic situation developed without warning. We don't know yet if it involves only that one laser cannon or if it's common to all the aircraft, but it's either a major problem with the system, or someone deliberately caused it. It's fifty-fifty, so I can't ignore the possibility of sabotage. I'll know more after I get the computer analysis."

"Call me immediately when you know something."

"Yes, sir, I will."

Joe sat back in his chair, his eyes thoughtful. Sabotage. No one ever liked to consider it, but he couldn't afford to discount it. Technology constantly created new techniques in spying and sabotage. The security police had gone to great lengths to keep Night Wing under wraps, which was why every entrance into every building, both doors and windows, contained sensors linked to a central computer that kept track or who was in each building at any given time, recording both entrance and exit times. Guards were also posted at the hangars at night and no one had approached the planes without proper clearance, but if the problem was sabotage, that meant only that the saboteur had the required security clearance.

If he were lucky, the laser team would find the problem and it would be something mechanical, something explicable. If not, he wanted to have the security check already in progress.

What a bitch. If they didn't find out what was wrong immediately, it would ensure that he wouldn't see Caroline tonight, and last night without her had been pure torment. It was amazing how quickly his body had become accustomed to frequent gratification, and how strong his sexual hunger for her was. He'd never wanted a woman that way before, like an incessant fever that refused to be cooled. He'd never enjoyed a woman that way before, without any boundaries or restrictions. She was vital and electric, as straightforward with her loving as her thoughts and personality were.

It had been a mistake to let his thoughts slip to her. His pants had become very uncomfortable. *Down, boy,* he thought wryly. Now was definitely not the time or the place.

No matter how they checked, they couldn't discover how the laser had been activated by accident. Caroline's actual expertise was with the laser itself, not with the triggering mechanism. That was Adrian's field, and he was surly because of it. If the problem was laid at his door, he might be recalled from the project or possibly even fired. Typically, he took out his frustration on Caroline.

"What are you, a jinx?" he muttered, scowling as he painstakingly checked every detail of the firing mechanism. "Everything was going fine, just a few minor kinks now and then, until you showed up. Things started falling apart as soon as you started working on them."

"I haven't worked on that mechanism," she pointed out, refusing to let him anger her or to get embroiled in a finger-pointing episode. She didn't have to say anything else, however, because Adrian took her comment to mean that he *had* been working on it, so therefore it was obviously his fault.

"Let's stop the bickering," Yates ordered. "Cal, is *anything* showing up on the computer?"

Cal looked exhausted, his eyes bloodshot from staring at a monitor screen and stacks of dim printouts for too many hours. He shook his head. "It's all checking out on paper."

They were standing grouped around the laser pod on the belly of the aircraft Bowie had been flying. Caroline stared at the pod, deliberately blotting out what everyone else was saying as she tried to sort things out. The laser seemed to be in perfect working order, as did the firing mechanism. The lock-on was also performing perfectly, but then, they already knew that. After all, it had locked on to Daffy's bird and blown it out of the sky. But what had *told* it to lock on? According to the computer record, Bowie definitely hadn't touched the switch, so the lock-on and firing mechanisms had both operated automatically, something they weren't supposed to do. Nor was the laser supposed to have been activated; actually firing the lasers hadn't been scheduled for another ten days. Three things had gone wrong simultaneously: the laser had activated, the lock-on had targeted Daffy's aircraft and the thing had automatically fired. None of those three things was supposed to have happened at all; for all of them to have happened at the same time went beyond chance or Murphy's Law.

She didn't like the direction her thoughts were taking. If it wasn't logical for those three things to have happened by accident, then they had to have happened by design. The laser couldn't be activated by an accidental bump, and it certainly didn't have an outside switch labeled On and Off. Activating the laser was something the laser team had to do with a precise set of commands to the computer. Because of the security involved, they were the only ones with access to those commands.

Inescapable logic indicated that one of the team had activated the laser.

Caroline didn't believe in leaping to conclusions. Her work habits were orderly and painstakingly precise. Before she let herself begin thinking that one of the three men she worked with was deliberately sabotaging the laser, she had to make certain there was no way anyone outside the team could do it. Everything was computerized now, and though safeguards were built into the programs and elaborate precautions taken, nothing was impossible. There were a lot of things so difficult that no one had done them yet, but that didn't make them impossible. It was feasible that if someone could get the activation commands, he or she could also get into the program and use them. And it would be child's play for anyone that knowledgeable about computers to add commands that would override the pilot's physical keying of the lock-on switch, say if another aircraft came within a certain distance. Maybe Bowie had been flying a ticking timebomb today, just waiting for the right set of circumstances. It had been Daffy's bad luck that he had been assigned to shadow Bowie, but it could as easily have been Mad Cat, or even Joe, who had been shot down.

Yates had been watching her thoughtfully for several minutes. She was standing motionless, her gaze locked on the pod but not seeing it, with all her concentration turned inward. He could almost see that computer brain running down a checklist and inexorably narrowing the possibilities.

"What is it?" he finally asked when he couldn't stand the suspense any longer. "Any ideas?"

She blinked, and her eyes slowly refocused on him. "I think we should check the computer program," she finally said. "If it isn't the equipment, it has to be the program."

Cal looked positively haggard. "Do you know how long it will take to check this entire program?" he asked incredulously. "This thing is huge. It's the most complicated program I've ever worked on."

"Maybe a Cray..." she murmured, looking back at the pod.

"Book time on a Cray supercomputer?" Yates made it a question, but he was already mentally running through the logistics. "Expensive as hell."

"Not as expensive as stopping the program."

"It could take forever to get a booking, unless the Pentagon can line up some priority time."

"Yeah, that's a fine idea," Adrian said impatiently, "but you people are forgetting that the big man gave us thirty-six hours, of which we have already used ten. I don't think he's going to be satisfied with a possibility."

"We've come up with nothing everywhere else. Do you have a better idea?" Caroline replied just as impatiently.

He glared at her without answering. The truth was, they had all reached a dead end.

Caroline didn't mention her other conclusion, that if

the solution to their problem was in the computer program they still had to discover whether it was a basic error in programming or if someone had deliberately programmed it in, but running everything through a Cray would give them the answer to that. By comparing the working program with the original, the Cray could tell them if the working program had been altered in any way. If it hadn't, then it was back to the drawing board for DataTech; if it had, then they had to find the person responsible for the changes.

"So what do we do?" Cal asked, rubbing his eyes. "Stop looking and just assume we're going to find it in the program, or stay up all night looking for something when we don't know what we're looking for?"

Despite herself, Caroline had to grin. "If you're as groggy as that sentence sounded, I don't think you *can* stay up all night."

He gave her a bleary look and an equally bleary grin. "Sad, isn't it? In my younger days I could carouse all night and work all day, then go back out for more carousing. What you see here is a shadow of my former self."

"I'm glad you two don't find this serious," Adrian snapped.

"Knock it off!" Yates ordered, temper in his usually calm voice. They were all tired and frazzled. He moderated his tone. "I mean it literally as well as figuratively. We aren't accomplishing anything except exhausting ourselves. We're calling it quits for the night, despite what I said earlier. I think we've eliminated everything it could be except the program, so that's our logical next step, and we can't do it here. I'm going to clean up and have a good meal while I think about this, then I'm going to have a talk with Colonel Mackenzie. Let's get some rest."

Captain Ivan Hodge, head of security, said without preamble, "We have a very suspicious pattern here, sir."

Joe's stern face showed no emotion, though he wished the captain hadn't found anything.

Major General Tuell's flinty eyes became even flintier. As base commander, he was ultimately responsible for everything that happened, and he was intensely concerned with whatever had caused the crash of an F-22. "Show us what you've found."

The captain was carrying a thick log. He deposited it on Joe's desk and flipped it open to a premarked page. "Here." He noted an entry he had already highlighted in yellow. "This is the security code number for a member of the laser team, Caroline Evans. She arrived last Tuesday as a replacement for a worker who had a heart attack."

Joe's guts knotted up and his eyes went blank as he waited for Captain Hodge to continue.

"She has a pattern of arriving in the morning before everyone else and being the last to leave," the captain said, and Joe relaxed a little. Caroline was a workaholic; hardly damning circumstances, and he himself had walked in on her unannounced several times, catching her doing nothing suspicious...although she had quickly cleared the computer screen that one time.

He had briefly wondered about it, then forgotten it, until now.

"You yourself have that pattern, sir," Captain Hodge said to Joe. "In itself, it doesn't mean anything." He flipped to another premarked page. "But here, on Thursday night, the sensors show Ms. Evans entering the laser work area shortly before 2400 and not leaving until almost 0400. She was alone the entire time. She reentered the building at 0600 for her normal workday. The birds went up that morning and for the first time experienced some malfunction with the lasers, isn't that right?"

The ice was back in Joe's eyes. "Yes."

"She left the area late that afternoon with the other members of the team and didn't return until Sunday night, again shortly before 2400. Again, she was the only person there. She left the building at 0430, returned at her usual time of 0600. This time, Major Deale's aircraft was shot down. Hell of a lot more disruptive than the lasers not working at all. These midnight appearances in the work area, combined with the fact that the trouble didn't start until she arrived, don't look good." The captain hesitated as he looked at Joe. The colonel's expression was enough to make any sane man hesitate, and Captain Hodge considered himself very sane. Nevertheless, it had to be said. "I understand you've taken a...uh, personal interest in Ms. Evans."

"We've gone out together a few times." They'd done a hell of a lot more than that, he thought savagely. She had given herself to him with a completeness that had shattered his memories of other women, reduced them to nothingness. And after they had returned from Vegas Sunday night she had slipped out to the work area and...done what? Secretly activated the laser on Bowie's aircraft? Had the laser on the bird he'd been flying been activated, too? Could he just as easily have been the one who shot down a friend?

Captain Hodge looked uncomfortable. "While you were with her, did she say anything? Ask any questions pertaining to Night Wing?"

"No." He was certain of that. Work had been mentioned in only the most general way. But then again, why should she have to ask him anything? "She has the clearance to find out anything about the project that she wants without having to ask anyone else."

"That's true. But did she say anything that, in retrospect, you could construe as being a reason for wanting the lasers to fail? Or for wanting to scuttle the Night Wing project?"

"No." But she wouldn't; Caroline was too smart for that. Caroline was brilliant. Caroline was perfectly capable of activating the lasers; she was not only an expert, she had access to the codes. "She has the knowledge and she had the opportunity," he heard himself saying. "Do you have anything else? Motive, anything suspicious in her past, any current money problems?"

"Her background is clean as a whistle," the captain admitted. "We're going to do a total recheck to make certain it's correct and none of it has been fabricated, but that's only a precaution. Everyone connected with this project has been verified down to the fillings in their teeth."

"Clarify this for me," Major General Tuell said. "She could activate the lasers from the work area, without actually being in contact with the lasers themselves? The birds are under twenty-four-hour guard."

"Yes, sir," Captain Hodge said. "By computer command. And Ms. Evans carried a double major in college. She got her doctorate in physics, but she also has a master's in computer sciences. She knows her way around computers."

"I see." The general sighed. "What are your recommendations?"

"We won't file formal charges, sir. We can prove opportunity, and the timing is very suspicious, but we haven't as yet proven that the computers have actually been reprogrammed to arm and fire the lasers. There's still a possibility that it's a mechanical snafu."

"But you don't think so?"

"No sir. The problems began when she arrived, and in both instances they occurred after she had made midnight visits to the work area. She's a civilian. I recommend that the FBI be notified and that she be restricted to base, but not yet taken into custody. As a precaution, I would also restrict the entire laser team from the work area until this is settled."

"Why is that, Captain?"

"As I said, sir, as a precaution. She may not be the only one involved."

"The logs don't show anyone else entering the work area at suspicious times."

"That doesn't mean they didn't know about it. I think Colonel Mackenzie will agree with me that it's less expensive to halt testing for a few days than to lose another F-22, or maybe even one of the prototypes."

"Yes." Joe's voice was hard. "Are you going to question Ms. Evans?"

"Yes sir."

"I'd like to be there."

"Of course, sir." Captain Hodge thought wryly that Colonel Mackenzie didn't have to have permission; he had supreme authority on this base with anything concerning the Night Wing project. He would defer to Major General Tuell, but it would be by choice.

"When?"

"I can have my people escort her here now, if you'd like."

"Then do it."

Major General Tuell stood. "Gentlemen, I'm leaving this in your hands. I trust you'll both make certain of our position before charges are filed. However, do whatever has to be done to solve this. The project is too important."

They both saluted, and he returned it. As he left, Captain Hodge gestured to Joe's telephone and said, "With your permission, sir."

Joe nodded curtly. Captain Hodge lifted the receiver and pressed a code. "Have Ms. Caroline Evans, C12X114, escorted to Colonel Mackenzie's office. Verify."

Whoever had answered the phone repeated the code number. Captain Hodge said, "Correct. Thank you."

He hung up the phone and turned to Joe. "Ten minutes," he said.

Chapter 10

Caroline had never felt so small and exposed and terrified. She sat in a chair in Joe's office and tried to catch his eye, to silently plead with him to believe her, but he wouldn't look at her. Or rather, he was looking at her all right, but it was with a cold, totally impersonal gaze, as if he were observing a bug. He wasn't seeing *her,* Caroline. It was the look on his face more than anything else that frightened her. It was as hard as stone.

"No, I did not reenter the work area on those occasions," she repeated for what seemed like the hundredth time.

"The sensors logged both your entrance and exit times, Ms. Evans." Captain Hodge, the head of base security, was also good at repeating himself.

"Then the sensors are wrong."

"No, the sensors are extremely accurate. State-of-the-art."

"The sensors are *wrong.*" She drew a deep breath, trying to calm herself. She felt almost sick with fear. "I dislodged my ID card somehow during the day Thursday. I discovered it was missing Friday morning when I dressed."

"So you keep saying. We have no record of you filing a report on this so-called missing card, and you realize, of course, how important this would be on a top-security project. Perhaps you would like to explain your reasoning again."

"I remembered snagging it on a file folder Thursday and thought it must have come loose then. I didn't notify security because it seemed like a lot of bother when I was fairly certain it wasn't lost but was still in the office."

"But the sensors record you leaving the building that afternoon with the other members of your team. You had to have had your tag on for that to be possible, and believe me, Ms. Evans, the security works on both entering and exiting. If anyone crosses that threshold from any direction without the proper identification, it triggers an alarm."

"And that's why I'm telling you that the sensors *have* to be malfunctioning. When I discovered that I'd misplaced my tag, I called Cal Gilchrist and got him to check the office for me. He found my tag lying on the floor under my desk. He brought it back out to me and returned to his quarters while I began work. All you have to do is ask him."

"Mr. Gilchrist will be asked the appropriate questions. However, what the logs show is that both you and Mr. Gilchrist entered the building together and left together two minutes later. Then you reentered alone, and it was over an hour before Mr. Gilchrist returned."

"That's impossible. I did *not* go into the building until Mr. Gilchrist returned with my tag. What do your precious sensors tell you when two tags but only one body leave a building?"

The captain ignored her question and instead made a quick notation on the clipboard he carried. "Did you also misplace your tag on Sunday night?"

"No. I didn't enter the building on Sunday night." She couldn't prevent herself from giving Joe another quick, imploring glance. What was he thinking? Surely he didn't suspect her of sabotaging the lasers.

"The sensors say you did. And by your own testimony, your ID tag was with you."

"The tag was exactly where I had left it Friday afternoon when I put it on again this morning."

"You didn't move it at all during the weekend?"

"I spent the weekend in Vegas."

"And left your tag behind."

"Do you wear *your* ID tag off-base, Captain?" she shot back.

He said mildly, "I'd like to remind you that I'm not the one under suspicion."

"Under suspicion of what? Spell it out for me," she challenged.

He refused to be drawn. "You spent all weekend in

Vegas, you say. You didn't return to the base either Friday night or Saturday night?"

"No."

"Where were you in Vegas?"

"At the Hilton."

"There's more than one. But of course this can be verified?"

Joe interrupted. "Ms. Evans and I spent the weekend together. I can verify her time from late Friday afternoon until 1900 hours Sunday."

"I see." Captain Hodge kept his voice noncommittal, but Caroline's face burned. This time she didn't glance at Joe. "So the name tag was locked in your quarters the entire time."

She tried another calming breath. They didn't seem to be working very well. "Yes."

"You're certain your quarters were secured."

"Yes. I always double-check my door."

He looked sceptical. "'Always' is a very exact term. It means without fail. Are you saying you've never failed to double-check your door?"

"On this occasion, Colonel Mackenzie himself checked the door while I watched."

The captain glanced at Joe, who nodded. Joe's eyes were hooded, his expression unreadable.

"You verify that the tag was in your possession and no one else's. You were recorded entering the work area at exactly—" he paused to check the log "—2347 on Sunday night."

"I was in bed at that time Sunday night."

"Alone?" the captain asked indifferently.

"Yes."

"No one can verify that. You say you were in bed. The computer log says you were in the work area."

"Talk to Cal Gilchrist!" she said fiercely. "Stop wasting time with this and verify what I've already told you."

"On Thursday morning, when I walked into your office you cleared the screen and turned the computer off," Joe said. His voice was cold and deep. "What was on the screen that you didn't want me to see?"

She stared at him in silence, completely at a loss. He sounded as certain of her guilt as Captain Hodge was, but surely he knew… She tried to concentrate, to bring the occasion to mind. Thursday morning. He had startled her yet again, she remembered, and when she had reflexively started to slug him he had jerked her into his arms. She remembered fiddling with the computer to give herself something to do while she tried to get a handle on her reaction to him, but she had no idea what she had been working on.

"I don't remember," she said weakly.

"Come on," he scoffed. "You remember everything. You have a mind like a steel trap."

"I don't remember," she repeated, staring at him. With a shock she realized that the expression in his eyes was one of disdain…disgust…even rage. Yes, it was mostly rage, but not the normal heat of temper. Joe Mackenzie's rage was ice-cold, and all the more frightening because of it. He was looking at her as if he could destroy her without regret. *He didn't believe her!*

The enormity of that realization almost choked her. As it was, a huge knot in her chest swelled until she could scarcely breathe, until her heart was beating with slow, painful effort. Had their situations been reversed she would have given him her complete, unqualified trust without hesitation, because, despite the evidence, she knew he would never betray his country. Evidently he believed her capable of doing just that. Her thought processes were orderly and logical, but all of a sudden a staggering instinctive knowledge filled her: she would trust him because she had been fascinated by him, intensely involved with learning about him as a man because she loved him, while for him their time together had been purely physical. He hadn't bothered to learn about her as a person because he didn't care.

In shock, she withdrew. She didn't move physically, but she had been reaching out to him mentally, and now she slammed her mind's door on those thoughts. She pulled all her reactions inward, bolting them inside in an effort to reestablish her emotional safeguards. It was probably too late, but the human animal's instincts were always to survive, and so she obeyed those instincts. Her face went smooth and expressionless, and she stared back at him with eyes as blank as glass. She couldn't afford to give him even a sliver of herself.

"What were you working on?" he repeated.

"I don't remember." Even her voice was flat. She had so desperately clamped down on her emotions that none of them stood a chance of escaping. Just as emotionlessly she said, "I'm going to assume I'm under suspicion of sabotage."

"We haven't said that," Captain Hodge replied.

"Nor have you said that I'm not, and this feels very much like an interrogation." She fastened her gaze on him, because she couldn't bear to look at Joe. She didn't know if she could ever look at Joe again. Later, when she was alone, she would regroup and take stock, do a damage assessment, but for right now she felt as if everything in her would shatter if she had to look at him. The pain was just too great; she couldn't handle it, so she had to ignore it.

"We couldn't find any malfunction at all in the laser on Captain Wade's aircraft," she said, and even managed a little bit of pride in the evenness of her tone. It was as flat as the EEG line of a corpse. "We all talked it over. Yates Korleski, the team leader, was going to talk to Colonel Mackenzie tonight after he'd thought about it a bit longer, but we think the problem is in the computer program."

Captain Hodge looked mildly interested. "What kind of problem are you talking about, Ms. Evans?"

"We don't know. We want to compare the working program with the original to tell us if any changes have been made on the program we're actually using."

"And if there are changes?"

"Then we find out what those changes are."

"Whose idea was it to verify the program?"

"Mine."

"What made you think of it?"

"It was a process of elimination. The computer program is about all that's left that *could* be wrong."

"But the program was working perfectly before you

arrived. It would be a major feather in your cap if you solved a problem of this magnitude, wouldn't it, Ms. Evans?''

She didn't flinch, just continued to stonily watch him. ''I didn't sabotage the program so I could have the glory of finding the problem.''

''I didn't accuse you of doing so. I merely asked if it would be a feather in your cap if you pinpointed a major flaw in a project this large and important.''

''I already have a good professional reputation, Captain. That's why I'm on the team.''

''But you weren't an original member, so evidently you weren't good enough for that. Did you resent not being picked in the beginning?''

''I didn't know about it, so I couldn't be resentful. I was working on something else. The Night Wing project was already in full swing before I finished my own project. I only became available a month ago. That's verifiable,'' she added before he could ask.

''Hmmm.'' He studied the notes he had on his clipboard a moment longer, then looked up with a thin smile that didn't reach his eyes. ''I believe that's all I have to ask you for now, Ms. Evans. You may go. Oh—you're restricted to the base. It wouldn't look good if you were caught trying to leave.''

''Are my telephone calls also restricted?''

''Do you need to call someone?'' he asked without answering her question. ''An attorney, perhaps?''

''Do I need one?''

He gave her that thin smile again. ''We haven't pressed any charges yet.''

He just had to put that "yet" in there, she noticed distantly, but it didn't affect her. "You aren't filing charges but I'm restricted to base. Let me remind you that I'm a civilian, Captain Hodge, not a part of the military."

"And let me remind you, Ms. Evans, that you *are* on a military base and this is a military matter. If necessary, we can hold you in the brig for the maximum length of time before charges have to be formally filed. A lot of this can be checked out by then, and you may be exonerated, but if you insist on spending the time behind bars, we can accommodate you."

"You've made your point."

"I thought I had."

Caroline got up and concentrated on her legs. She made certain they didn't wobble, that they moved when she told them to. She didn't look at Joe as she walked out of the office, or at burly Sergeant Vrska on duty in the outer office. Evidently the good sergeant left only when the colonel did.

They would talk to Cal, and he would verify everything she had told them, which would force them to accept that their precious security sensors could and had malfunctioned. Perhaps there had been a major foul-up in security and two ID tags had been issued with the same bar code. Perhaps someone had been entering the work area with a duplicate of her tag and had indeed been sabotaging the computer program, but questioning Cal would force them to admit that it wasn't her.

She wasn't worried about being charged with sabotage, though enduring the captain's questions hadn't been a pleasant experience. But she might never recover from the look in Joe's eyes and the realization that he didn't trust her, that he believed her capable of sabotage.

She had made a monumental, colossal fool of herself. Despite the superior capability of her brain, she had made the fundamental feminine mistake of assuming that making love with a man signaled a commitment from him. No, not making love, having sex. That was another mistake she had made, assigning too much importance to the act. To men it was the simple gratification of a physical appetite, like eating. No emotional baggage was involved. She had made love; he had had sex. She had given herself to him, heart, soul and body, and he had given her pleasure in return but nothing of himself beyond the temporary use of his own body. Magnificent as his body was, she had wanted more. She had thought she was getting more.

Oh, she hadn't gone so far as to think he was in love with her, but she had still thought he *cared,* at least a little. But she had been confusing sexual technique with emotions. He had none, at least none that she could reach. He was always controlled, his inner self firmly locked away from everyone except his immediate family. She was beginning to see the wisdom of that. Right now she would give anything if her own emotions had been that protected, so she wouldn't be about to collapse and curl up in a fetal knot from the pain of it. She would do so if she thought it would ease the pain, but she knew it wouldn't. There was no ease.

Perhaps when he knew the truth he would expect to continue their affair as if nothing had happened. Caroline tried to imagine how she would handle the situation if he did, but she simply couldn't bring anything to mind.

Nor could she imagine continuing to work here, seeing him every day. She had always been right, after all, never to become involved with anyone. The first time she had done so had certainly been a disaster. So now she either had to do the unthinkable and somehow manage to survive working with him, or she had to ruin her professional reputation by asking to be taken off the project.

It looked as if her work would be all she had, so she'd be damned if she would throw that away just because of a man, even if that man was Colonel Joe Mackenzie. If it took every ounce of strength she had, she would finish this damn project. She would talk with him about work. She would even be polite. But there was no way she would ever risk opening her heart to him again. She simply couldn't afford the pain. This was already costing her almost more than she could bear, and the ordeal had just begun.

''Cal Gilchrist categorically denies finding her ID card under her desk,'' Hodge told Joe later. It was almost midnight, but there was no possibility of sleep in sight. ''He says she called him early Friday morning and asked him to walk her to the building because she thought someone had followed her the morning before and it made her nervous. He says he also went inside with her for a quick check of the building, then returned to his quarters to shower and shave."

Joe's face was stony. He hadn't allowed himself to hope that Gilchrist would verify everything she had said. It would have been asking for too much, when the sensors had plainly placed her there when she shouldn't have been.

"Then why use him for an alibi? She must have known he wouldn't cover for her."

"Maybe not. Evidently they're fairly good friends. Certainly Adrian Pendley wouldn't have gone a single step out of his way for her. And maybe she and Gilchrist had something going on in the past, for her to feel confident he would protect her if he could."

"No." At least he was certain about that. Caroline had never been intimate with anyone but him. Before Ivan could question him on his certainty Joe asked, "What about Korleski? Did they discuss the possibility that the problem was with the computer program?"

"Yes. She told the truth right down the line with that. He verified that she's the one who suggested the program be checked. He was also vehement that she wouldn't sabotage a project so she could have the credit of saving it. Neither did he believe she would do it for money."

"Did he think anyone else on the laser team *would* do it for either money or prestige?" Joe asked.

Ivan shook his head.

"How do the rest of them check out?"

"It'll take time to reverify everything, but all of

them are spotless. I never would have suspected her if it hadn't been for the entrance and exit records.''

Joe could understand that. He never would have suspected her, either, but then, he hadn't been able to see past his own obsession with her. All he'd been able to think about was getting her in bed and burying himself in that sweet body. Now he had to wonder how much of it had been calculated, if she had indeed been so attracted to him that she'd given up her virginity to him with hardly a thought or if she had done it… God, what possible reason *was* there for making love with him the way she had, other than desire? No, she hadn't come on to him in an attempt to find out classified information on Night Wing or to use him for protection if she were caught. She hadn't needed him to find out anything; she had access to all the information she wanted. And it was simply too iffy to assume he would protect her just because he'd slept with her. Caroline had wanted him. Even if he couldn't trust anything else about her, he could trust that.

So what did he do now? He'd never before been so enraged and…hurt. He might as well admit it. This had been like taking a roundhouse to the gut. Nobody had ever gotten to him the way Caroline had, with her uncomplicated fierceness. She had been forthright and brutally honest, without any hidden agenda or stratagems. He wanted to be able to step back from the situation and look at it without emotion, but he couldn't.

He'd never felt about any aircraft the way he felt about Night Wing. It was special. It was more than special. It was history in the making, pure magic in the air. He would give his own life unhesitatingly to protect those planes, because they were necessary to protect his country. Simple patriotism, pure love for those birds. They were *his.*

And he'd considered *Caroline* his, too. His woman.

If the choice had been simply between Caroline and the aircraft, he would have chosen Caroline. He might despise himself for it, but he couldn't have stood by and let her be harmed. But between Caroline and his country... There was no choice. There couldn't be. He couldn't let there be. No matter how fierce and gutsy she was, no matter how she challenged him on a level no one else ever had before and threw herself without restraint into the battle. She hadn't let him be gentle when he'd taken her for the first time; she had insisted on receiving his full strength and had met him with her own. Caroline met life head-on, without wavering.

He paused in his thoughts, a tiny frown puckering his eyebrows. Caroline didn't seem the type to sneak around in the dark. Maybe he hadn't known her as well as he'd thought, but he would have sworn there wasn't a devious bone in her body.

He wanted to see her. He wanted to ask her some questions one on one, without anyone else in the room to buffer them. He would get the truth out of her come hell or high water.

Chapter 11

He had intended to go straight to her quarters, but he stopped halfway there and detoured to his own quarters in the BOQ instead. He was too angry to face her now, especially in the temporary civilian housing where there would be too many onlookers who didn't need to know any of what was going on.

He didn't think he'd ever been this angry before, but then, he'd never been betrayed like this before. Damn it, why would she do something like that? It had to be money, but he'd never understood the mentality that could view treason as just another financial opportunity.

Treason. The word reverberated through his consciousness. If she were charged and convicted, she would likely spend the rest of her natural life behind bars, without possibility of parole.

He would never make love to her again. The thought made him erupt with fury, and he restlessly paced the small confines of his quarters. One weekend hadn't been enough. He doubted that a thousand weekends would be enough to get her out of his system. Nor could he let himself forget that he had made love to her twice without protection. Despite her assurances that the timing was wrong, she could be pregnant.

Hell, what a mess! If she was pregnant... There wasn't any use in borrowing trouble; he'd know soon enough. But what would he do if she was carrying his child? There still wasn't any way he could keep her out of prison.

That was assuming she would even tell him. By the time she had left his office that night she had refused to even look at him. He'd been watching her, trying to read her reactions, and all of a sudden she had started withdrawing. He'd seen it happen right in front of his eyes. It was as if a light had been quenched. All the vitality, the responsiveness, the incredible energy of her, had vanished, and all that had been left was a frozen mannequin of a woman who had answered in a monotone and whose eyes were as blank as a doll's.

It had been infuriating to see her that way. He had wanted to jerk her to her feet and shake her, to make that wonderful, uncomplicated anger come rushing upward to meet him. But he hadn't. If he gave in to those urges, he would lose his control once and for all, and he never wanted to do that.

What he did want to do, more than anything else in the world, was storm over to her quarters and make love to her so hard and so long that when it was over she would know she belonged to him. Maybe it wouldn't solve any of this, but it would sure as hell make him feel better. But he couldn't do that, either. Seeing her at all would knock down the last critical brick behind which he had dammed up his temper, releasing a flood of emotion that would sweep him away along with everything else.

Caroline lay on top of the covers on her narrow mattress, too listless to crawl between the sheets and actually go to bed. Such a normal action was beyond her. She had showered and dressed for bed, but she couldn't even go through the motions of pretending to sleep. All she could do was lie there in the silent darkness and stare at the ceiling. She could feel her heart beating, feel the slow, rhythmic expansions of her rib cage as she breathed. Those actions said that she still lived, but she didn't feel alive. She felt numb, dead inside.

By now they would have talked to Cal, who would have verified that she'd been telling the truth. Joe would know that he'd been wrong, but somehow that didn't give her any satisfaction. Still, she had expected at least a phone call from either him or Captain Hodge, to say "Sorry, we made a mistake." Surely they wouldn't be stupid enough to think she was *resting* and would rather they wait until morning to tell her.

Or Cal could have lied.

She couldn't deny the possibility. The thought had slipped into her consciousness not long after she had lain down on the bed. If she hadn't been so upset, it might have occurred to her earlier. It was the natural progression of the line of thought she had been following earlier in the hangar, when she had been staring at the laser pod and sorting out the various ways in which what had happened could have happened.

Cal was a whiz with computers. He was the one who had found that minor glitch on Friday, but only when Caroline had begun nosing around the computer. She hadn't thought anything of it then, but if he had tampered with the commands, he wouldn't have wanted her to really concentrate on the program. He knew she had a degree in computer science, because they had talked shop on several occasions. And on both Friday and today—yesterday, now, since it was past midnight—he had really looked exhausted. From being up all night? Cal was normally as bouncy as a rubber ball.

And Cal was the only other person who had touched her ID tag. Maybe he had picked it up on Thursday when she'd lost it and had left when she had so that the sensors would match the number of warm bodies leaving with the number of ID cards. She hadn't known the sensors monitored those leaving the buildings, too, but maybe Cal had; after all, he'd been working here from the beginning and noticed things like that, while she tended to pay attention only to what directly concerned her job.

Even if he had used her ID tag to regain entrance to the building Thursday night, she knew he hadn't had it on Sunday night.

But how easily could they be duplicated? He would have had to leave the base to get it done, but she was certain it was possible. After all, the sensors had said she had reentered the work area at midnight, which would have given him several hours to have a copy made.

Then she had called him on Friday morning asking him to search the office for her tag, which had given him the perfect opportunity to return it to her and keep security from being notified. Otherwise he wouldn't have been able to use the card again, because security would have removed that particular code from the computers.

She stopped her thoughts and rubbed her forehead, trying to force everything into making sense. If her call for help had been pure chance, then there wouldn't have been any reason for him to have had the card duplicated. Had he played the odds that she *would* call *him?* They were good odds, she had to admit. She wouldn't have called Yates, and she certainly wouldn't have wasted her time calling Adrian. It was also a good bet that she wouldn't have wanted to call security. Not a certainty, but good enough that it wasn't much of a risk, either.

So what had happened then? The sensors showed both her and Cal entering the building, then both leaving. He must have had her card on him where the sensor could read it, thereby establishing proof that he hadn't had the opportunity to tamper with the computer program because he hadn't been in there alone. But why hadn't the sensor noticed that there were two cards but only one body?

Maybe the sensors weren't as good as Captain

Hodge obviously liked to believe they were. Maybe they were programmed to catch people without cards, but no one had thought to program it to catch cards without people. Maybe Cal had figured out a way to fool it. There were a lot of maybes, all of them possible. As good as he was with computers, maybe he had somehow gotten into the base computers and logged her both in and out of the building that morning. She didn't know and might never find out.

But what would Cal do now, if he were guilty? If the programs had been tampered with, he would know that analysis would discover it. Would he try to get back into the program and cover his tracks by undoing what he had done, hoping that the analysis wouldn't go any further than a simple comparison? Or would he try to plant more evidence against her?

She had to go with the second option. It was so much more feasible. Why would Cal go to so much trouble only to undo it? No, as long as the finger was pointing toward her, he would be smart to try to make certain it remained pointing in that direction.

Her heart suddenly began thundering in her chest. If Cal were guilty, if he were going to do anything else, he would have to do it *tonight,* while things were still in an upheaval. Given enough time, the security net would settle down so tightly that nothing would be able to escape, but there were still windows of opportunity when things first started happening.

She knew the entire laser team was being restricted from the work area, but had their bar codes already been deleted from the computers? The military worked a lot like big business when it came to office work: most of it was done during the day. Since the restriction order had only been issued that night, had Captain Hodge called in someone to enter it into the computer or left it to be done first thing in the morning? Knowing human nature, she would bet on the latter. After all, she was the only one under suspicion, and she was probably under surveillance in the interim.

On a hunch she rolled out of bed and silently walked to the small, old-fashioned crank-out window set high in the wall in the kitchen area. She had to stand on a chair to see out of it. Sure enough, a security police car was parked on the opposite side of the street. In the glow of the streetlight she could plainly see two men in the front seat. They were making no effort to disguise their purpose, but then, why should they? This wasn't clandestine surveillance, but plain old guard duty.

There was no other door.

There was, however, another high, narrow window in the bedroom. In the almost total darkness she carefully made her way back to the bedroom and stared at the small oblong of light in the wall. A man certainly couldn't get through there, and she had doubts that she could, either. Nevertheless, she stood on the bed and peeped out. That side of the street was empty.

Well, there was no point in putting herself to a lot of trouble if Cal was peacefully sleeping in bed. She mustn't let herself forget that he might be totally innocent, that he had indeed verified her story. Innocent until proven guilty was the law of the land, though

Captain Hodge could use a little refresher course in the concept.

She didn't want to turn on any lights, alerting those two out front that she was awake, so she dialed Cal's number by feel. What better way to find out if he was in his quarters than to call him? If he answered, she might even chat awhile.

By the fifth ring she began to have serious doubts that he was there. She let it ring longer, just in case he was sleeping very soundly, but on the twentieth ring she replaced the receiver. Twenty rings, especially since the phones were installed right beside the beds to make certain the occupants would be awakened by any middle-of-the-night phone calls, would wake even the soundest of sleepers. Cal wasn't in his quarters.

She clenched her teeth in anger. Damn him! She had thought he was her friend; she had liked him, trusted him. First Joe, now Cal. Her mind immediately shied away from Joe, because that hurt was too powerful to linger over. It was much safer to focus her anger on Cal.

She stared up at that little window again. Two long, narrow louvered panes that cranked out to let the built-up heat of the day escape. She would have to dismantle the entire mechanism in the dark, and even then, she wasn't certain she would fit through the slot.

Well, she would never know if she didn't try.

Working on lasers and computers had made her familiar with tools, and she never traveled anywhere without a small pouch containing a selection of screwdrivers and pliers, because she never knew when she would need them. She fetched the pouch from the closet and dumped the tools out on the bed. Problem was, in the dark she couldn't tell which tool she needed.

She did have a pencil flashlight and decided she would have to take the risk of the small beam being detected through the window, but it wasn't likely to throw a lighted patch on the ground outside and alert the guards. She climbed up on the bed and switched the flashlight on for only the smallest of intervals, just long enough for her to see that the screws holding the mechanism in place needed a Phillips head screwdriver. Five minutes later the two window slats and the cranking mechanism, in pieces, were lying on her bed.

That had been the easy part. Getting through the window was something else.

She measured it visually. She could angle her shoulders through; her head and hips would be the biggest problem, but her buttocks would compress and her skull wouldn't. She decided to go headfirst, so she could find out immediately if her head would fit through. It would be awful to go out feetfirst, then be stuck with her head inside and the rest of her body outside. Humiliating, at the very least. That is, if she didn't find herself hanged.

First, she had to change clothes and put on some shoes. She shone the pencil flashlight on the contents of her closet, taking care that no light was visible from the outer rooms. Dark clothes would be practical, but she hadn't brought any dark clothes with her. It was

August in the southern Nevada desert; she hadn't anticipated being obliged to sneak around in the dark.

She would stand out like a sore thumb in her light-colored clothes, but there wasn't any help for it. She would just have to make certain no one saw her.

Nevertheless irritated by her lack of preparedness, she quickly pulled on a pair of thin cotton pants and a T-shirt, and defiantly slipped her ID tag into her pocket. If she got caught, they wouldn't be able to say she didn't have proper identification. As an afterthought, she added her keys to her pocket. She could hardly reenter by the window, though if she managed to catch Cal up to no good, she wouldn't have to worry about the guards out front.

She climbed up on the bed again, but a minute's experimentation made it plain that she needed to be higher so she could angle through from a more horizontal position. She got a kitchen chair and balanced it on the bed, then climbed up on the chair. It was a wobbly perch, but she was holding on to the edge of the window and wasn't afraid of falling.

One arm and shoulder went first, then she turned her head to the side and eased it through the slot, earning nothing more horrendous than a minor scrape. She wiggled the other shoulder and arm through and braced her arms on the wall below her as she wriggled forward. As soon as her hips were through, she suspected, her center of gravity would shift drastically forward and she would fall on her head, dragging her legs the rest of the way through the window. It wasn't a high drop, but she didn't want to break her neck landing.

To prevent it, or at least slow her down, she hooked her legs backward so her heels were braced against the inside wall, and inched forward some more.

The edge of the window cut into her soft bottom but she ignored the pain and forced herself on through. Immediately she lurched forward and only her hooked legs inside kept her from doing exactly as she had feared. Frantically, she braced her arms again, forcing herself as far away from a vertical position as possible, then cast a fearful glance toward the front of the building where the guards were parked. To her relief, she couldn't see the car from where she was.

She hung there a minute before she faced the inevitable: there was no graceful way to do it. She was going to be scraped and bruised. Moreover, there was no way she could now reverse the process and inch back inside. Her legs were trembling from the strain. Without giving herself time to dwell on how much it was going to hurt, she straightened her legs and gave a push with her arms at the same time, launching herself the rest of the way out of the window. She tried to turn in midair so nothing vital was damaged on landing, like her head, and succeeded in turning mostly to the side. The impact was harder than she ever would have suspected for such a short distance. The loose gravel scraped skin on her temple and cheek, down the side of her left arm and on her left ankle. She had banged both knees somehow, and jarred her shoulder.

But she couldn't just sit there and take stock of her injuries. Her senses were still swimming when she forced herself to move, to scramble against the shadows at the side of the building and walk quickly in the opposite direction. Only when she had gone almost a hundred yards without hearing a warning shout did she relax and take a deep breath. Immediately her pains made themselves felt, and she stopped to lean over and rub both aching knees, then her bottom. She rotated her shoulder to make certain it was in working order and gingerly touched the side of her face. She didn't seem to be bleeding, but the scrapes burned. A scarf threaded through the loops of the pants usually served her as a belt, but she stripped it out and carefully blotted the scrapes to remove the dirt and tiny bits of gravel from her face.

Something else she could lay at Cal's door.

She trudged the long way around, no longer making an effort to avoid being seen on the theory that someone would be more likely to notice her if she was trying not to be noticed. If she acted normally, no one would pay any attention to her.

Joe sat up and threw the sheet off, cursing steadily under his breath even as he got up and began dressing in jeans and boots. It wasn't military business he had to attend to, and the long, restless hours in a bed that was far too empty had steadily eroded his patience until there was none left. He glanced at his watch, surprised to see that it was only about 0200 hours. He'd been in bed less than two hours, but it had felt more like four or five. It didn't matter. No matter how long it had been, he wasn't going to be able to sleep until he'd had it out with Caroline. He wanted to hear her explanation of why she'd done what she had, and he wanted her to tell him to his face. He wouldn't let her ignore him again the way she had earlier in his office.

He decided to walk rather than take the truck for the relatively short distance; maybe the walk would settle him down. He was dangerously close to exploding, and he knew it. He had been six years old the last time he'd lost his temper, and he'd sworn then never to do it again, but Caroline tested his control to the extreme.

He'd walked less than a quarter of a mile when he first saw the slim figure walking boldly through the night, and his first thought was that temper was making him hallucinate. He stopped and stepped back out of sight, going down on one knee next to a trash can. He hadn't mistaken her identity; the overhead streetlights gleamed on her pale hair, and he knew that walk as intimately as he knew his own face. The arrogant set of slim shoulders, the gentle sway of rounded hips, were burned into his memory.

Was she coming to see him? His heart thumped wildly, but then he wondered how she had gotten past her guards. He knew they had been there, because he had suggested to Hodge that it would be a good idea, and Hodge had agreed. He'd even heard Hodge give the orders. But here she was, walking around the base at two a.m., not a guard in sight.

He waited until she had walked past him before slipping from his cover. As always, he moved soundlessly, dropping back about fifty yards but always keeping her in sight. If she turned toward the BOQ he could rapidly close the distance and approach her. But she didn't even pause at the BOQ, and his anger rose to the boiling point. She was headed straight for the laser work area, damn her treacherous little heart. His palm itched with the almost irresistible impulse to storm up behind her, take her by the nape of the neck and bend her over his knee. By the time he got through walloping that pretty little backside he would feel a lot better and she would have a better appreciation of just how angry he was. Damn it, didn't she know how serious her situation was?

Of course she did. By her own actions, she was proving herself guilty. Probably she intended to finish the traitorous work she had already begun.

He thought of stopping to alert the security police, but decided in favor of keeping her in sight. If she tried anything like setting the place on fire he could subdue her and hold her until security got there. In fact, he would *enjoy* subduing her. He just might get that walloping accomplished while they were waiting.

He saw her stop and get something out of her pocket, then attach it to her shirt. Her ID tag. Why hadn't Hodge relieved her of it? Because he hadn't seen any need to; she had been under guard, and the codes would be deleted from the computer first thing in the morning. Joe was suddenly furious again, but this time at both Hodge and himself. They had been inexcusably lax, especially for a project with security as tight as Night Wing. She couldn't get off the base, but she could still wreak havoc *on* base. They relied too much on technology to do their guarding for them, something he intended to change immediately.

Someone was already inside the building; there was a very dim glow coming from one of the windows, barely noticeable. Caroline saw it, too. He saw her head turn as she stared at the light; then she continued straight up to the door and slipped inside, as silent as a wraith.

Twenty seconds later, he followed. He wasn't wearing his ID tag, so he knew central security would be alerted immediately.

Up ahead, he saw Caroline reach into the office and flip on the light switch, bathing her in the bright light. "What did you do, use my name tag again?" she demanded furiously of someone else inside. "The computers will probably go crazy when they record Caroline Evans entering twice in a row. You sabotaged my project, damn you!"

Realization burst in his brain like a bomb, and shock slammed through him as she stepped completely inside the office, out of sight. Damn the little idiot! She didn't have one iota of caution. She had simply charged straight in without thinking that cornering a traitor could be dangerous. Joe launched himself down the corridor, running silently, desperately praying with every fiber in him that he wouldn't hear a gunshot that would mean the end of that foolhardy courageousness.

He heard a sudden movement, a gasp, a sickening thud, and he burst through the open doorway just as Caroline slid to the floor. Cal Gilchrist was standing in front of a glowing computer monitor, his face utterly white. Too late Joe saw Cal's eyes dart to the side, behind him. He tried to whirl, but he'd been too distracted by his own unreasoning fear. Before he could react, something hard crashed against his temple. It felt as if his head was exploding. Then there was nothing but total blackness.

Chapter 12

Caroline slowly regained consciousness, at first aware only of being jounced uncomfortably. Her head hurt with a deep throbbing that dulled her senses, but gradually she became aware of pain in her shoulder and arms, too. Then she began to realize that she could hear voices, that there was someone else near her, but for a blank, frightening moment she didn't know who or where she was.

Then she recognized one of the voices, and awareness swept through her. She remembered everything. Cal. It was his voice she recognized, and just as she realized that, she also realized that she was in a vehicle of some sort, perhaps a van, and she was tied. Gagged, too, damn it.

Slowly she opened her eyes, quickly closing them again in pain when a bright light flashed quickly through the windows. She heard a rushing sound and realized some other vehicle had passed them on the road, nothing more. She tried again, this time opening her lids only a slit so she could accustom herself to the discomfort. This must be what a hangover felt like, and she hadn't even indulged. All the misery without any of the fun.

Someone was lying beside her.

This time she closed her eyes in panic, startled by the realization that there was a man right next to her. She was acutely aware of her helplessness. Oh, God, were they going to rape her?

But the man wasn't moving. Cautiously she opened her eyes one more time and found herself staring straight into Joe Mackenzie's pale, furious eyes.

Even if she hadn't been gagged, she couldn't have said a word, she was so astonished. How had he gotten there? She had a good idea how *she* had come to be in such a predicament, because she had foolishly rushed into the office to confront Cal without making certain he was alone. But how had Joe gotten involved? Then fear swelled in her chest, because he was in danger, too.

"I say we forget about it and get out of the country," Cal was saying feverishly. "It's over. I can't take it any further. They're going to check the entire system, and they'll find everything."

"I told the others you didn't have the nerve for this," someone else replied dismissively. Caroline tore her gaze from Joe's and craned her neck so she could see up front. Another man was sitting beside Cal, who was driving. She didn't recognize him, but at the same time he looked vaguely familiar.

"Nothing was said about murder," Cal replied furiously.

"And I suppose if that pilot had died when his plane was shot down, you wouldn't have been responsible for that?"

"That was different." Despite his words, Cal's tone was uneasy.

"Yeah, sure."

"That was...chance. But this is cold-blooded murder. I can't do it."

"No one's asking you to do it," the other man said impatiently. "You don't have the nerve for it. We'll take care of it. Don't worry, you won't even see it happen."

If her hands hadn't been tied behind her back, Caroline would have lunged for the man, she was so angry. He was talking about killing them as casually as he would talk about doing the laundry! Joe silently nudged her ankle with his boot; actually, it was more of a kick, and her ankle was already sore. She turned her glare on him, and he gave a tiny, warning shake of his head. She kicked him in return, and he blinked at the pain.

They were in a van, one which was evidently used for hauling cargo rather than people, for there was no carpeting on the floor, only bare metal. The vehicle swayed with every turn, curve and bump, adding to the discomfort of her position. She was lying on her sore shoulder anyway, and having her hands tied behind her made it worse.

She tried to discern what they had used to bind her; it felt like nylon cord, while it was probably her own scarf they had tied around her mouth, adding insult to injury. Her keys were still in her pocket. If she could get them out, and if she and Joe turned so their backs were to each other, and if they had enough time, she might be able to use the edge of a key to saw through the nylon. The keys weren't sharp, but they were rough. Joe's pockets had probably been searched for a knife, a common item for men to carry, but women weren't expected to carry anything in their pockets, and evidently Cal and his cohort had totally overlooked hers.

"There's no point in killing them," Cal was saying raggedly. "It's over. We barely got out of there before the security police started swarming all over the place. By now they know I left the base, and they have a record of the van's license plate. When Caroline and the colonel are both reported missing but neither of them is recorded as leaving the base, they'll put two and two together so fast there'll be an APB out for the van within another hour, at most. Right now we're looking at life, but if we kill them, we'll get the death penalty."

To Caroline that sounded like a very convincing argument, but the other man didn't seem impressed. He didn't even bother to respond.

Sometimes she wished she weren't so darn logical. She couldn't turn off her thought processes even when they were telling her something she would rather not know. If the other man disregarded Cal's argument, then it must be because he had some reason to believe he himself wouldn't be tied in to the sabotage. As Cal had pointed out, his own involvement was known, but this other guy must think himself safe...except Cal knew about him and could tie him to everything. Therefore, the man felt safe only if he knew that Cal wasn't going to be alive to make the connection.

Furiously she began rubbing her face against the floor of the van, trying to scrape the gag away from her mouth, pushing against it with her tongue at the same time. Joe glared another warning at her, but she ignored him. Her frantic movements attracted the attention of the man in the passenger seat up front, and he turned around.

His voice was genial. "Welcome back, Ms. Evans. I hope your headache isn't too bad."

Joe had closed his eyes again and was still lying motionless. Caroline made an angry noise, muffled by the scarf, and continued her struggles. She kicked her bound feet and twisted her torso, all the while fighting the gag.

"You might as well stop wasting your time," the man said in a mild, faintly bored tone. "You can't get free, and all you're doing is pulling the cord tighter."

She wasn't concerned about the cord. Her two aims were to get the gag off and somehow dislodge the keys from her pocket. Not an impossible task, since her pants were loose, flimsy cotton, but not an easy one, either, because the pockets were deep. She mumbled a few unintelligible curses at him and continued with her struggle.

She had managed to push the scarf out of her mouth, and on an impulse she scooted over next to Joe and pushed her face hard against his shoulder, using the contact and the friction between his shirt and the scarf to roll the gag downward. Joe didn't move, and his eyes remained closed. She worked her jaw until the gag slipped down to hang around her neck. The man in the front seat was frowning at her, starting to get up on his knees and twist around.

"You dirtbag, you've killed him!" she croaked, forcing as much rage as possible into her voice, even though her tongue and jaw didn't want to work.

The van swayed alarmingly as Cal jerked on the wheel, his head swiveling around to stare into the back. The other man fought for his balance. "Keep your eyes on the road!" he barked at Cal.

"You said he was just unconscious!"

"He isn't dead, damn it. I hit him harder than I did her because I didn't want any trouble with the big bruiser if he woke up before we could get them out of there and tied up."

Caroline yelled, "Cal, he's going to kill you, too! Why else wouldn't he be worried about a murder charge unless he's going to try to blame the whole thing on you?"

The man lunged at her from over the seat, reaching back to grab her around the throat. Quick as a cat she turned her head and sank her teeth into his arm. He howled and tried to jerk back, but she hung on like a limpet, working her jaws to inflict as much damage as possible.

The van was swerving all over the road. Cal was using his right arm to grab at the other man while still driving. Both men were yelling and cursing. Suddenly the other man used his right fist to club her on the side of the head and she saw stars, her jaws going slack as she helplessly sank back. She didn't lose consciousness, but the blow definitely addled her.

They were fighting in the front seat, and the van rose dangerously on two wheels; then Cal jammed on the brakes and it slewed violently to one side, sliding off the pavement. She felt the distinct difference between pavement and dirt; then the van tipped a little to the right as it came to rest, probably in a shallow ditch. The movement threw her against Joe, and she felt his muscles tense as he took her weight, but he didn't so much as even grunt. Instead, there was an almost soundless, barely intelligible whisper against her ear. "There's a knife in my right boot."

Well, of course there was. Didn't all colonels carry knives in their shoes? Furious because he managed to be armed when she couldn't even get her keys out of her pocket, she thought about biting *him,* too. Instead, she hurled herself toward the rear of the van, collecting even more bruises in the process. Cal and the other man were still grappling, and she caught a glimpse of something metallic gleaming in the other man's hand. Instinctively she recognized it as a pistol.

Cal somehow got his door open and leapt out, probably figuring he didn't have very good odds in such close quarters with a pistol. The other man was swearing viciously, steadily, as he shoved open his own door and went in pursuit.

Caroline rolled around so her back was to Joe's feet, searching by feel for his right boot, struggling to push his pants leg up so she could reach the knife. They wouldn't have long, probably less than a minute. Her scrabbling fingers, numbed from the tightness of the nylon cord, finally grasped the knife handle and drew it out.

Joe was already rolling, presenting his bound hands to her. It wasn't easy to position the knife between their backs, unable to see if she was slicing into flesh or nylon, but she figured Joe would let her know when she got to skin. The knife must have been sharp; within five seconds she felt the cord give and he was rolling away from her again and sitting up. The blade was removed from her numb hands. She twisted her head to see him bending forward to quickly slice the cord around his feet; then he whirled toward her. She felt a swift tug at her hands and they came free. Before she could even bring her arms around he had jackknifed to a sitting position and freed her feet. Only then did he remove his own loosened gag, tugging it down so it hung around his neck just the way the scarf hung around hers.

A shot boomed from in front of them.

"Stay back here," Joe ordered as he lithely swung into the front and folded himself behind the steering wheel. The engine was still running; he slammed the van into gear and stepped on the gas pedal. The wheels spun uselessly, and he cursed himself even as he let up on the gas and put the transmission in reverse, this time easing down on the gas. He was used to his truck, but the van didn't have that kind of traction. The tires clawed for purchase on the loose, shifting dirt, finally caught and reversed out of the rut he'd dug with the first effort.

In the beam of the headlights he could see the second man running back toward the van. There wasn't any sign of Cal.

Caroline's head popped up beside him as he shifted into first, and simultaneously the man stopped and lifted the pistol. Joe put his hand on Caroline's head and shoved her sideways as he ducked himself, just as the pistol boomed again and the windshield shattered, spraying shards of glass all over the interior of the van. He kept his foot on the gas pedal and his head down as the van leapt out of the slight depression and skidded when the tires touched asphalt, slewing sideways again. He fought to keep the vehicle upright.

More shots, one following immediately after the other. He could feel the impact of the heavy slugs on the van. One headlight went out. Briefly he saw the man pinned in the remaining headlight; then the guy jumped sideways to safety as the van roared past.

"Caroline!" he shouted, needing to know if she was okay, but he had his hands full battling the van, the wind full in his face and blinding him now that the windshield was gone, and he couldn't turn to see.

"What?" she shouted in reply.

"Stay down, he might shoot—"

Before he could complete the sentence, bullets

ripped into the rear of the van, shattering those windows, too. His blood went cold.

"Caroline!"

"What?" she roared, plainly aggravated, and he could have laughed with relief. If Caroline was in a bad mood, she was all right.

The relief didn't last half a minute. A quick glance at the gauges showed the engine's temperature was quickly climbing; one of the shots must have hit the radiator. They were out in the desert somewhere, without a sign of a town, community or even a lone dwelling. The only light was from the stars and their one headlight. They wouldn't be able to get far before the engine locked up, but he intended to put every foot of distance that he could between them and the man with the gun.

The temperature gauge redlined. He kept his foot on the gas pedal.

The engine locked with a harsh, grinding sound. Caroline shot up beside him as they rolled to a stop. "What's going on?"

"Some of those shots hit the radiator. The motor's gone. Come on, out of the van."

She obeyed, pushing the sliding side door open and staggering out into the cool desert night. "Over here," Joe ordered, and she made her way painfully around the van.

"Now what?"

"Now we walk. I hope you're wearing good shoes."

She shrugged. She was wearing loafers, not as good as boots, but better than sandals. She hadn't dressed with an odyssey like this in mind, but what did it matter? She had to walk, even if she'd been barefoot.

"In which direction?"

"Back the way we came."

"*He's* back there."

"Yeah, but we don't know where we are, or how far it is to even a gas station going in the direction we were heading. At least we know that if we go back the way we came, we're going at least roughly toward the base."

Logical. But… "If we're going back the way we came, why didn't you drive in that direction to begin with?"

"Because then he'd *know* what direction we were going in," he explained. "He'll find the van, but he won't know if we continued on ahead or doubled back."

"But obviously we're going to have to pass by him at some point."

"Very possible, but not a dead certainty. He may decide to run rather than try to catch us. Since we don't know, we have to assume he's after us."

She trudged silently beside him as he walked out into the desert. They didn't dare risk walking on the road, so that meant they had to parallel it, far enough from the roadside that they couldn't easily be spotted, but close enough that they wouldn't lose sight of the pavement. She ached in so many places that it didn't seem worth the effort to worry about any of them. They had to walk, so she walked. It was as simple as that.

"Are you wearing a watch?" she asked. "What time

is it? It isn't dawn yet, so they couldn't have taken us far.''

Joe tilted his wrist to read the luminous dial. ''It's four-thirty, so it'll be dawn soon. If they just threw us in the van and left immediately, before the security police could close the base, we're talking at least an hour of driving time. We could be anywhere from thirty to sixty miles away from base.''

Walking sixty miles was a daunting thought, but not nearly as daunting as facing that man again. ''There are others,'' she said aloud. ''Maybe close by. They could have been taking us to turn over to them. It'll be dawn soon, but we don't dare try to flag anyone down, because we don't know who the others are or what they look like.''

''You got it,'' he said grimly.

''So we have to walk every foot of that blasted sixty miles.''

''Unless we see a state trooper. At least when the sun comes up I'll have some idea where we are.''

Too far away from anything to suit her. She stopped talking, partly because sound carried so far in the desert and she didn't want to alert anyone to their presence, but mostly because it was taking all her effort just to walk. She had been awake all night—except for when she'd been unconscious, but she was fairly certain that didn't qualify as rest—and she was exhausted. Her head pounded. She supposed Joe's head hurt, too, but he'd only been hit once. First she had tumbled out her window, then she'd been hit on the head, probably with the pistol, then with that guy's fist, and finally she had hit her head against the side of the van when Joe had shoved her. The wonder was that she had any sense left at all. She ached in every muscle of her body, and a good many of the bruises adorning her had come at Joe's hands. She was glad she'd kicked him back and only wished she had gone ahead and bitten him, too. She hoped he had the granddaddy of all headaches.

Twice he drew her down when a noise alerted him. She never did see anything, but he had superior eyesight, so she let him do the work while she seized the opportunity to rest. When he decided it was safe to continue on he would urge her to her feet with an implacable hand under her elbow, and she would walk some more.

Dawn began to turn the sky pearly to their left, giving them the basic information that they had been carried north into the desert and were now headed south, back toward the base. She supposed it was good information to have, in case they had to lose contact with the road.

"We can't go on much longer," Joe murmured in her ear. "Anyone passing will be able to see us from the road, and it'll get too hot to walk, anyway. We need to find shelter for the day."

She didn't like the sound of that. It was safer to stay hidden and sleep during the day, walking only at night, but it was sure going to take them a long time to get to the base. If she hadn't been so tired she could have argued, but she was beginning to feel incapable of going another foot, and she suddenly realized just how much the night's events had taken out of her. They simply had to rest.

He veered sharply away from the road, deeper into the desert. The light slowly changed to gray, letting them see details but not yet color. A huge rocky outcropping loomed in the distance, and she stared at it in dismay. That was almost surely where he was going, and she wasn't certain she could make it. She ground her teeth to keep from protesting. She either made it or she took a nap in the sun, which would soon be broiling. She was also thirsty, but they had no water, so there wasn't any point in bringing it up. He had to be thirsty, too.

When they finally reached the rocks she leaned thankfully against one huge boulder. "Now what?" she gasped.

"Stay here."

He was already gone, vanished into the rocks. She mumbled, "Sure," and sank down to the ground. Her temples were throbbing. She closed her eyes and leaned her head against the stone behind her.

It felt as if she had no sooner closed her eyes than he was saying, "Come on," as he ruthlessly hauled her to her feet. He pulled her higher up into the rocks and shade enveloped her. Until then, she hadn't realized how quickly the desert had heated. He'd found a niche in the rock deep enough to provide protection for both of them, and he deposited her in the crude shelter.

"I've already checked for snakes," he said as he put a stick in her hand. "But if any show up, knock them away with this. I'm going to wipe out our tracks and find something to drink."

Automatically she closed her fingers around the stick. She knew she should be uneasy at the thought of snakes, not to mention watchful, but she had more important things to do right then, like sleep. She turned over onto her right side, because it hurt the least, and immediately dozed.

Joe stared down at her, his jaw muscles flexing. The left side of her face was bruised and scraped, and so was her left arm. He could plainly see a lump on her temple. She was chalk white with exhaustion and pain, her clothes dirty and sporting a few small tears. The contrast between her normally pristine appearance and now, when she lay bedraggled at his feet, sleeping in the dirt, utterly enraged him. Cal Gilchrist was probably dead, but he wanted the other one dead, too, for what they had put her through. He himself hadn't done a very spectacular job of keeping her safe, and he included himself in his rage.

She looked so small and helpless, curled on her side like that, though he knew she wasn't exactly helpless. He remembered her furious struggle to free her mouth from the gag so she could yell her suspicions at Gilchrist; she had caused the fight between the two men, thereby engineering their own escape. It was up to him now to make certain nothing else happened to her.

His own fatigue pulled at him as he backtracked for quite a distance, then obliterated all sign of their passing on his return to the outcropping. He ignored the weariness of his muscles. They needed water; not desperately, not yet, but they would stay much stronger if they had adequate liquids. Before he let her get dehydrated he would take the chance of flagging down a car, but it hadn't come to that yet, and he didn't want to take unnecessary chances. With an expert eye he noted the stunted plant life dotting the desert floor, studying the growth pattern and picking out the plants that looked slightly more succulent than others growing nearby and indicating more moisture underground. They would be all right.

He climbed back to the niche in the rocks. Caroline hadn't moved; she was breathing with the slow, heavy rhythm of deep sleep. Suddenly it seemed like a lifetime since he had held her, felt her nestling trustingly in his arms, and one moment longer was too long. He lay down beside her and eased her into his arms, cradling her head on his shoulder. She sighed, her soft breath brushing his skin.

Damn her, why hadn't she called him, told him of her suspicions about Gilchrist? It had been obvious that she wasn't surprised to find the man in the work area, had in fact gone there specifically to find him. She had barged straight into danger rather than picking up the telephone and calling him, or even Hodge. All of this could have been prevented if she'd just made that call instead of trying to do things herself.

That would be the first thing he got straightened out between them when she woke up. Why the hell hadn't she trusted him? If he had to tie her to the bed every time she was out of his sight to keep her from rushing headlong into dangerous situations, he would do it. He remembered the black terror he'd felt, seeing her dart into the office to confront the saboteur, and he wanted to shake her until her teeth rattled.

Instead he held her tighter, smoothing her pale hair back from her face. He could feel her heart beating against his, and right now that was all he required. He slept as easily as she had, simply closing his eyes and letting weariness sweep over him in a tide.

Chapter 13

It was the heat that woke her. She felt rested, her headache having subsided to a distant and far more tolerable ache. Slowly she sat up, staring out at the glaringly hot landscape stretched before her, wavering in the heat: reds in every shade, yellows, browns, sand colors. Small specks of green that testified to the sparse plant life. Beautiful. Basic. Cal was probably dead somewhere out there, and despite what he had done, what he had tried to do, she couldn't help but mourn him. He hadn't wanted to kill them, had argued against harming them. Poor Cal. He'd been a traitor, but not a murderer, though what he'd been doing could easily have led to someone's death. Poor Cal. But if Joe had been harmed because of him, she would have killed him herself.

Sweat stung her eyes, and she dried her face on the

arm of her shirt. If it hadn't been for the sheltering rock, the heat would have been intolerable. She reached out and touched the stone, found it cool to the touch. Where the sun kissed it, it would fry eggs.

Joe wasn't there, but she wasn't alarmed. She had a vague impression that he'd been lying beside her, and the imprint in the dirt confirmed that. Probably he had disturbed her when he'd gotten up, and that had allowed the heat to intrude on her consciousness.

She felt incredibly grubby, and looking down at herself, she saw that she *was* incredibly grubby. She didn't think she'd been this dirty since…come to think of it, she'd never been this dirty before. She had been a fastidious child, eschewing the joys of mud puddles for those of computers and books.

Stiffly she climbed to her feet, wincing as her various aches made themselves felt. Aching or not, nature called.

When she returned to the niche, she found Joe leaning propped against the rocks, looking disgustingly capable. His eyes were piercingly alert, and even though his clothes were as dirty as hers, they looked made to be dirty. Jeans and a khaki shirt were far more utilitarian than thin white cotton pants and an oversize white T-shirt. Even his scruffy boots were better suited to the desert than her loafers; she had to be careful how she stepped, to avoid getting the fine silt inside her shoes, where it would promptly rub her feet raw.

After a single encompassing look that avoided meeting his gaze, she stepped past him and sank down in the shade of the rocks again.

Joe's back teeth ground together. He'd thought he had himself firmly in control once more, but all of a sudden he was right back to where he'd started, dangerously close to the precipice. She was shutting him out, damn it, and he found it intolerable.

Grimly he regulated his breathing, forcing his hands to relax, his jaw to unclench. She was still fragile from the rough handling she'd had the day before; now wasn't the time to force a confrontation, even if he had been sure of his control, which he wasn't. Later. He promised himself full satisfaction—later.

"We both need something to drink," he finally said. "Come on."

Unhesitatingly she got to her feet without any sign of her usual argumentativeness, which had to mean she was very thirsty.

They didn't have far to walk; Joe had already scouted the area and marked the most likely spot in a small arroyo, where the scrub grew profusely. He knelt on the sandy bottom and began scooping up the sand with his hands. It quickly grew damp. He slipped the knife from his boot and dug deeper, until muddy water began to gather in the hole.

His gag had been made from a handkerchief, and it came in handy now. He spread the square of cloth over the water to filter the liquid, then gestured for her. "Drink."

Caroline didn't take exception to his curt tone; he had produced water, and that was the important thing. She didn't cavil about unsanitary conditions or the indignity of having to get on her hands and knees and lap liquid like a dog. It was water. She would gladly stand on her head to get it if it was required. She could feel the membranes of her mouth and throat absorbing the tepid moisture, and it was wonderful.

Still, she forced herself to stop long before her thirst was quenched and moved away from the tiny water hole. She gestured to him. "Your turn." She didn't know how much water there was; there might be only enough for both of them to have a few swallows each.

He stretched out full length on the sand to drink, which she considered and decided was a far more comfortable position. She should have thought of it herself, but then, she had never lapped water from a puddle before. She would know next time. Absently she studied his prone figure. As big as he was, it stood to reason that he had more blood in his body than she did, so he would probably require more water. Biology had never been one of her interests, but she would bet he had at least one more deciliter of blood than she did, perhaps two. An interesting little tidbit she needed to investigate…

She blinked and became aware that he had risen to his feet and was waiting, having evidently asked her something. "Do you want more water or don't you?" he repeated impatiently.

"Oh. Yes, thank you." This time she stretched out as he had done, which gave her better access to the small puddle of water. She sucked enthusiastically until she began to feel as if she'd had enough. She paused to ask, "Have you finished, or do you want more?"

"I've had enough," he said.

She soaked the handkerchief as best she could, then gingerly washed her face and hands, wincing when the water stung the scrapes. When she had finished, she offered the handkerchief to Joe, and he scrubbed the damp material over his own face and hands, and around the back of his neck. The moisture had a cooling effect, something he needed right then.

"We'll wait in the rocks until sundown," he said, and she nodded. Without another word she headed back to the protective niche.

Damn it, she was treating him like some stranger she'd been stranded with. No, even worse than that. She would have talked more to a stranger. She hadn't once looked him in the eye. Her gaze would slide past his face without connecting, as if he were someone she passed on the street. His hands clenched into hard fists as he strode after her. It was time to have it out, damn it.

She was sitting on the ground in the niche when he got there, her arms looped casually around her drawn-up knees. Joe deliberately walked so close that his boots nudged her feet, forcing her to either stand up and face him or tilt her head back as far as it would go. She continued to sit.

"Why the hell didn't you call me last night instead of tackling Gilchrist on your own?" he asked softly, so softly it would take a discerning ear to catch the quiet fury underlying the words.

Caroline heard it but didn't much care. She shrugged. "I didn't think of it. I wouldn't have, anyway. Why would I?"

"So I could take care of it. So you wouldn't nearly have gotten yourself killed."

"And you, too," she pointed out. "How *did* you get involved?"

"I was following you."

"Ah." She gave him a brittle smile. "Thought you'd catch me in the act, didn't you? What a surprise to find out it was someone else who got caught."

"And you knew it when you went there. Damn it, Caroline, for such a smart person, that was a stupid thing to do. You should have called me when you first suspected him."

"Yeah, sure. Why waste my breath?" she asked scornfully. "I'd already seen how much you believed me. I'd rather have called Adrian Pendley than you, and he hates my guts."

His breath hissed softly between his teeth as he leaned down and grasped her arms, jerking her unceremoniously to her feet. "If you ever need anything," he said, the words deliberately spaced as he forced them out, "you call *me.* My woman doesn't go to someone else."

She pulled sharply, trying to dislodge his grip on her arms, but he merely tightened his hands. "Interesting, I'm sure," she snapped. "When you find her, be sure to tell her that, but *I'm* not interested."

A red mist swam in front of his eyes. "Don't push me," he heard himself say hoarsely. "You're mine, damn it. Admit it."

Again she tried to pull away, her blue-green eyes spitting fire at him. If he thought he could just pick up again where they had left off, now that it had been proven to his satisfaction that she was worthy, he was in for a nasty surprise. She wanted to scream at him, but instead she limited herself to a scathing retort. "We had a hot weekend in bed, but that doesn't give you a deed to me. Boy, were my eyes opened. I knew you weren't madly in love with me or anything, but you really can't have much of an opinion of someone at all if you think they're capable of betraying their country. It was certainly a learning experience—"

"Shut up." His voice was guttural now.

"Don't tell me to shut up," she fired back. "The next time I go to bed with a man I'll make certain he—" *"You'll never go to bed with any man but me."* He began shaking her, the force of it whipping her head back and forth. The thought of her turning to another man was unbearable, shattering the last tenuous thread of his control and letting rage spew forth like lava, red-hot and molten. She was his, and he was never going to let her go.

Somehow his mouth was on hers, his hand locked in her hair at the back of her head, holding her still. He tasted blood, whether his or hers he didn't know, but the coppery taste called up a fiercely primitive instinct to brand her as his, sear his flesh into hers so she would never be free of him. His skin felt burning hot and too tight, as if it would burst from the force of his blood pounding beneath it. His manhood was iron hard with lust, straining against the front of his jeans.

He carried her to the ground, blind with the need to feel her soft body beneath him. He began jerking at her pants, tugging them down and off. Her underwear tore when it was subjected to the same treatment.

Caroline lay still, staring in mute fascination at his face. She had always sensed his control and resented it, but abruptly it had shattered, and the naked intensity of his expression was almost frightening. Almost, because in the deepest, most basic part of her, she trusted him not to hurt her. She saw the savagery of his eyes, felt the barely restrained strength of his hands as he stripped her clothing away, and his wildness called her own fierce spirit soaring up to meet him.

She heard herself give a wild cry; then her hands were buried in his thick black hair, pulling him down to her.

He tore at the fly of his jeans, grunting as he freed his rigid length. He entered her with a powerful, driving thrust that made her cry out again from the impact of it; then her legs came up to hold him in the cradle of her hips as her silky hot depths wrapped around him, yielding, caressing, demanding. The sensation made him feel as if his skull was going to explode.

He rode her hard, grinding her into the hard ground beneath them in his frenzy to irrevocably meld their flesh into one. He'd never felt so savage, so utterly dominant and primitive; he was out of control, reacting purely as a male animal who needed his mate more than anything else in the world.

Caroline lifted her hips to meet his heavy thrusts. She had been sucked up into the maw of a powerful storm, and she loved it, reveled in it, embraced it and wanted more. The pleasure exploded in her, hard and deep. She clutched his hair, her heels digging into the backs of his muscled thighs as her slim body arched in a powerful bow, lifting him with her. The rhythmic surge rolled through her like thunder, and she gave herself up to it with a cry.

Her completion called up his own, the exquisite milking sensation on his hard length sending him over the edge. He convulsed with a powerful jetting that emptied him but seemed to go on forever, longer and harder and deeper than he'd ever known before. He was barely conscious when it ended, barely able to move. He didn't have the strength to roll away from her, or even to support his weight on his arms. He sank down onto her with the dim wish that he would never have to move, that they could lie there entwined for the rest of their lives.

He *needed* her for the rest of his life. He'd always loved flying with a passion that had overshadowed what he'd felt for other women, but right from the start he'd found it impossible to put Caroline out of his mind as he'd always been able to do once he was in the cockpit. She would never make a comfortable wife, but hell, if comfort and placidity were what he wanted, he would never have become a fighter pilot. He'd never been in a fighter yet, not even Baby, that kept him on his toes the way Caroline did. She both delighted him and challenged him, and she met the strength of his sexual drive with matching strength. He was a warrior, and she was as fierce as he was, with more guts than brains, and that was saying a lot. In more ancient times she would have fought beside him, a sword in her own hand. His Valkyrie. He felt humbled by her spirit.

"I love you," he said. He hadn't known the words were there until they came out, but he wasn't surprised by them. Somehow he found enough strength to surge up onto his elbows, looking down at her with his savage, glittering eyes narrowed. "You're my woman. Don't ever forget it."

Caroline's eyes flared, the pupils expanding to huge black circles that almost completely swallowed the vivid color of her irises. "What did you say?" she demanded.

He thrust his hips against her, deepening the invasion of his still-firm male flesh. God, how could he still be aroused? He was almost dead from exhaustion, but the want, the need, was still there. "I said I love you. And you're mine, Caroline Evans. Forever and a day. 'Til death and beyond."

"In sickness and in health," she prompted; then suddenly tears welled and overflowed, trickling down her temples.

He cradled her head in his hands and caught the tears with his tongue, tenderly nuzzling against her. His own chest felt tight. He'd never imagined his valiant little warrior crying, and it was almost more than he could bear. "Why the tears?" he murmured, pressing light kisses across her face and neck. "Did I hurt you?"

"You nearly killed me," she replied. "When you didn't believe me." And she balled up her fist and punched him on the side of the head, because it was the only place she could reach. It was an awkward punch, because of their closeness and her position, and didn't pack as much power as she would have liked, but he gave a very satisfying grunt. "Don't let it happen again."

He jerked his head back and glared down at her. "Why in hell did you do that?"

"Because you deserved it," she said, and blinked back another tear.

Joe's mouth twitched, and the glare turned into something tender. "I'm sorry," he breathed, feathering a kiss on each corner of her mouth. "I'm sorry. I was a blind, bull-headed ass. Just the suggestion that you might have betrayed me sent me into a flat spin, and I couldn't pull out of it. I was on my way over to see you when you came marching toward me, right down the middle of the base like you owned it, when you were supposed to be under guard." A quick frown knitted his brow, and he pulled back a little to scowl at her. "How *did* you get out?"

"I dismantled the glass slats in the bedroom window and crawled out."

He looked astounded. "You can't fit through there. It's too little."

"Hah. I got some scrapes from it and hurt my shoulder when I fell, because I had to go out headfirst, but it can be done." Then she judiciously added, "Though I don't think you would fit through even if you were greased from head to foot."

"Or any other man on base," he said dryly.

"Well, times have changed," she pointed out. "The security police should realize that women are a permanent part of the Air Force, even flying fighters into combat now, so they should adjust their thinking.''

Typical of Caroline to point out the security police's errors in letting her escape. He would be sure to pass them on to Hodge. If he beat Caroline to it, that is.

She gave a delicate little cat yawn, and her dark sea-colored eyes looked sleepy. Still, Joe was reluctant to disengage their bodies, though she was lying naked with nothing beneath her but the hard ground. He solved the problem by anchoring her hips with a hard arm and rolling so he was on bottom. She made a soft sound of contentment, very like a purr, and nestled her head into the hollow where his neck and shoulder met.

He leisurely stroked her slim back for a minute, then abruptly his hands tightened, and he lifted her off his chest to give her a hard look. ''What about you?'' he demanded sharply. ''Do you love me, Caroline? Say it.''

''Yes, sir, Colonel,'' she murmured in response to the commanding tone. She supposed it was something he couldn't help. ''I love you, Colonel, sir. Stupid of me, wasn't it, to fall in love when you were so determined to hold back, to not give me anything more than sex?''

Tension pulled the skin tight across his cheekbones, starkly revealing the chiseled bone structure. He felt the nausea of panic coiling in his stomach, because suddenly he saw that Caroline would never tolerate that rigid control, doling out passion and love in measured amounts. She wanted all of him. A cliff yawned at his feet, and if he stepped over the edge his life would never be the same, but if he didn't take that one step, he would lose her. He knew it all the way down to his bones, and just the thought of it was a hammer blow to the chest that told him he would never be able to survive the reality. His instincts were too sharp, too primal, for him to think he would be able to shrug it off. She was his mate; there was no other for him.

Somehow he forced his lips to move, though they felt numb. "I...I need to be in control."

He felt her hand on his hair, gently stroking, her soft fingertips trailing down to his cheek and then to his lips. "I noticed," she said, softly wry.

It was hard to explain, impossible with her lying on top of him, so close that she couldn't miss even the most minute change in his expression. He lifted her off him, though his body felt abruptly incomplete without the linkage to hers. She looked disoriented by the sudden shift, automatically crossing her arms over her bare breasts in response to her inner uncertainty. The gesture was so innately feminine that he grabbed her to him, holding her close and savoring the feel of her silky skin, gathering his strength. He brushed the dirt from her back, took off his shirt and slipped it on her. Her own clothes, he saw, were a tangled mess.

He kissed her, hard and quick, before tension drove him to his feet. He stood with his back to her, staring out over the stark, lovely desert.

"Dad was put in prison when I was six years old," he said. His voice was hoarse and raw. "He was innocent. The guy who had committed the crime was finally caught for something else, and he admitted everything. But Dad spent two years in prison, and for those two years I was in foster homes.''

There was total silence behind him, but he sensed the intensity of her attention. ''Maybe there was just something about me that the man in the first home hated. Maybe it was because I'm a half-breed. They kept other foster kids, but he singled me out. I was just a kid. I broke things, I'd lose my temper playing with the other kids, the way kids do. I was bigger and stronger than most kids my age, but I didn't know how to control that strength. If any of them said anything about Dad being a dirty half-breed jailbird, I went at them and did as much damage as I could. God, did I have a temper.

''And this man would beat me whenever I did something, even if it was stumble over an ashtray that he'd left on the floor. At first he used a belt, but it wasn't long before he was using his fists. I fought him, and he beat me that much worse. I missed more school than I attended, because he wouldn't let me go to school with my face bruised up.''

It got harder to say, the memories blacker as he dredged them up, and the worst was yet to come. He made himself continue. ''He kicked me down the steps once, broke a couple of my ribs. And still I kept fighting him. I guess you could say I didn't have stopping sense, but my temper flashed like black powder, and I couldn't control it. He started burning me with cigarettes if I sassed him, or twisting my fingers, just to see if he could make me cry.

''I was in a nightmare and I couldn't get out,'' he

said softly. "Nobody seemed to care what happened to me. I was just a half-breed, worth less than a mongrel dog on the side of the road. Then one day he slapped me, and I really lost my temper. I went on a rampage. I kicked in the television set, threw all the little knick-nacks against the wall, got in the kitchen and started breaking the dishes, and he was right behind me, hitting me with his fists, trying to kick my ribs in. I lost, of course. I was only six, even if I was big for my age. He dragged me down to the basement, stripped me naked and beat the bloody hell out of me."

His heart was pounding now, just as it had been that day almost thirty years before. He'd never said it before, but it had to be said now. "Then he raped me."

He could hear the swift movement behind him, feel the rush of air as Caroline surged to her feet. He kept his back turned.

"Looking back, I think it shocked him that he'd done it. He never touched me again, even in the slightest way. And I never lost control again," he said remotely. "He must have called the welfare people, or maybe his wife did. I was gone from that house within two weeks. I spent those two weeks in the basement, alone, silent. I stopped talking. The other foster homes were okay, I guess, but I didn't take any chances. I did exactly what I was told, never lost my temper, never lost control, never talked. Then one day, when I was eight, Dad showed up. He'd gotten out of prison and tracked me down. I don't know if he had authorization to get me or if no one was brave enough to tell him he couldn't, but he picked me up and held me so close it hurt, and it was the best hurt in the world. I was safe again."

"Did you tell him?" she asked, the first time she had spoken. He was a little startled at the harshness of her tone.

"No. I've never told anyone, until now. If you knew my dad, you'd know why. He would have gone after the guy and literally killed him with his bare hands, and I couldn't stand to lose Dad again." He steeled himself to turn and face her, braced for the pity he would see in her eyes, but what he saw was a long way from pity. She was standing with her fists clenched, her face savage with rage. If that long-ago man had been standing there right then, Caroline Evans would have killed him, too. She wasn't a half-breed Comanche warrior, but her spirit was just as swift and fierce, and her sea-colored eyes were blazing. Startled, he began to laugh.

"Don't laugh, don't you dare laugh!" she roared. "I'll *kill* him—"

"You don't have to, sweetheart," he soothed, jerking her into his arms when she evaded his more gentle attempts to embrace her. "He's dead. He died two years after the welfare people took me away. After I had graduated from the Academy I decided to check, just for the information. Hell, who am I kidding? There's no telling what I would have done if he'd still been alive."

He pushed her hair away from her face and kissed her. "Maybe I was tougher than most kids, but he didn't damage me permanently, except for always wanting to be in control. He didn't warp me sexually. Being around Dad was probably the best therapy I could have had, as far as sex is concerned. He was always totally open about it, treating it as just part of nature. And we had the horse ranch. A kid learns the basics damn fast on a ranch. I was okay within six months of getting back with Dad. There was a bedrock of love there that never let me down."

"Except you're still a control fanatic," she growled.

He had to laugh again. "You can't even lay all the blame for that on what happened. I'm a fighter pilot. My life depends on being in control. It's part of my training as well as my personality."

She nuzzled her face against his sweat-dampened chest. "Well, you have a reason for it, but that doesn't mean I like it."

"No, I don't guess you would," he said in amusement. "That's why you continually push me, trying to make me lose control. Well, lady, you succeeded. Are you pleased with yourself?" His voice turned deep and serious. "I could have hurt you, sweetheart."

She looked like the cat who had had an entire gallon of cream, not just a measly saucerful. "It was *wonderful*," she purred. "And I wasn't frightened. You can't hurt me by loving me. The only way you'll ever hurt me is if you stop loving me."

His arms tightened around her. "Then you're safe for a lifetime." He held her close for a long, long time, and he felt something relax within him, something that he hadn't even known was tightly wound. She was inside his defenses now, and he no longer had to keep his guard up. Defeat had never been sweeter, because he'd come away with the grand prize.

At the moment his grand prize was bruised and half-naked, but still valiant. He released her with a little swat to her bare backside. "Get your clothes on, woman. It's sundown, and we have to get back to the base."

Chapter 14

It was almost anticlimactic. The danger the night before had been very real, but it wasn't long after dusk when they veered back close to the road and a car came by, cruising very slowly, shining a spotlight off to the side. Caroline gasped and started to hit the dirt, but Joe kept her upright with a firm grip on her arm. His eagle eyes had spotted something she couldn't make out in the darkness: the row of lights on top of the car. Literally dragging her in his wake, he strode out into the road.

The car stopped. The spotlight wavered, then settled on him. "I'm Colonel Joe Mackenzie, out of Nellis," he said. His deep voice carried that unmistakable note of command. "I need to get back to the base as soon as possible."

The state trooper switched off the spot and got out

of the car. "We've been searching for you, sir," he said in a respectful tone. Military personnel or not, there was something about Joe Mackenzie that elicited that response. "Are you all right, injured in any way? A van was found—"

"We know about the van. We were in it," Joe said dryly.

"We were ordered by the governor to give every assistance to the military in finding you. A statewide search was started this morning."

Joe put his arm around Caroline and ushered her into the back seat; then he went around and took a seat up front. Caroline found herself staring at the back of his head through steel mesh.

"Hey," she said indignantly.

Joe glanced back and began to laugh. "Finally," he said, "I've found a way to control you."

"The sensor alarms went wild," Captain Hodge said. "Once when Ms. Evans entered the work area after she was already recorded as being inside, and again when you entered without your ID tag, Colonel. The first guard was there within two minutes, but the building was empty. They must have dragged both of you out immediately and then panicked. They loaded you in Mr. Gilchrist's van and bolted.

"Ms. Evans' quarters were checked and she was discovered missing. Amazing. I didn't know anyone could get out a window that small," he said, glancing at her.

"I'm not very thick," she replied coolly.

He cleared his throat at the look in her eyes. "I tried

to notify you, Colonel, and found that you were missing, too, though there was no record of you leaving the base. Nor had Ms. Evans attempted to leave. There was a record, however, of Mr. Gilchrist leaving immediately after the alarm had sounded.''

''The other guy must have been hidden in back with us,'' Joe said.

''Who was he?'' she asked. ''He looked familiar, but at the same time I didn't know him.''

Hodge looked at his ever-present clipboard. ''His name was Carl Mabry. You'd probably seen him in the control room. He was a civilian working with the radar.''

''How did Gilchrist get involved with him?'' Joe asked. ''And there are others. Have you found out anything about them?''

They were sitting in his office. Both he and Caroline had been checked over by the medics and declared basically sound. Somewhere along the line, Caroline's clothes had vanished and the well-meaning nurses had tried to stuff her into one of the too-revealing backless, shapeless gowns that were standard for every hospital. Caroline's sense of style had been outraged, but the green surgicals had appealed to her. She was wearing a set now and somehow looked dashing in them.

''Evidently, Gilchrist was recruited after he began work here,'' Hodge said. ''Mabry belonged to a radical group that opposed defense spending. You know the type. They want the money for humanitarian purposes, even if they have to kill to get it.''

"Then just how," Caroline asked in an awful tone, "did he get security clearance?"

Hodge winced. "I—uh, we're still checking on that. But he didn't have clearance into the laser building."

"So how did he get in without triggering the alarms?" Joe asked impatiently.

Caroline snorted. "The program has a major weakness. The alarm is set off by a body entering or leaving without a card—but not a card entering or leaving without a body."

Hodge's hair was too short to pull, so he ran both hands over his crew-cut head. "What?" he almost yelled.

"Well, it's obvious. I certainly didn't go into the building with Cal when he was supposedly searching for my tag, but the computer said that I did, which means he must have had the tag with him and flashed it so the sensors would pick it up, thereby destroying any record that he had entered the building alone and discrediting my story of having misplaced my tag. There wasn't anything Cal didn't know about computers. He probably figured it out not long after he started work on base, testing it by swinging the tag through the doorway on a string, or something like that. If he'd been caught, he wasn't doing anything he would be arrested for, just playing with the computers like any hacker would. Evidently he picked up my tag when I lost it, but left at the same time I did that day so the sensors weren't set off. He carried it off base and had it duplicated, then returned the original to me the next morning so there wouldn't be a report on it. The night we caught them—'' She paused, looking confused. ''When was it? Just last night?''

''Seems longer, doesn't it?'' Joe commented, grinning at her.

''Anyway, he would have entered with the duplicate tag, then tossed it through the doorway to Mabry, who would also have used it to enter. If you check the logs, you'll probably find entry, exit, then reentry with just a few seconds between. *If* you had been on your toes, Captain Hodge, you would have made certain my code had been immediately deleted from the computer instead of waiting until morning, thinking you had me safely under guard.''

Hodge was crimson with embarrassment. ''Yes, ma'am,'' he mumbled.

''Likewise, instead of assuming you had the problem contained, the entire laser team should have been restricted to base until you were certain.''

''Yes, ma'am.''

''The sensor program needs to be rewritten. It's humiliating to think of a sophisticated security system being bypassed by two people tossing ID tags through a doorway like kids playing catch.''

''Yes, ma'am.''

Joe had covered his mouth with his hand to hide his grin, but his blue crystal eyes were shining. Poor Hodge, by-the-book person that he was, was no match for Caroline at her most haughty, and his little hedgehog was most definitely feeling put upon. He decided to intervene before the captain was reduced to a sense of total inadequacy. "You used the past tense when speaking of Mabry. Is he dead?"

"Suicide. Gilchrist, by the way, was doing it for the money, not for any ideological reason, but Mabry firmly believed that the Night Wing program should be scrapped. They intended to cause so many problems with the tests that funding wouldn't be granted. Good plan, considering the economic and political climate. Pressure is high in Washington to spend money only on things that *work.* We've tied Mabry to a group called Help Americans First. I don't know if we'll be able to implicate any of them without his testimony, but we might be able to turn up a paper trail that ties them to it. We know they were willing to kill both you and Ms. Evans to complete their sabotage of the lasers, so we aren't talking about innocent do-gooders here."

"I want them nailed, Hodge," Joe said softly.

"Yes, sir. The FBI is working on it."

Caroline yawned. Despite sleeping all day, she was tired; it had been an eventful twenty-four hours. Joe leaned back in his chair and hooked his hands behind his head, watching her. It gave him a deep sense of contentment to watch her.

"You're the first to know, Hodge," he said lazily. "Ms. Evans and I are going to be married."

To his amusement, a look of disbelief crossed the captain's face. Hodge looked at Caroline the way he would have looked at a wild animal that had suddenly been turned loose, as if he didn't know whether to run or freeze. She returned the look with a sort of warning indifference.

"Uh...good luck, Colonel," Hodge blurted out. "I mean—congratulations."

"Thank you. And I'll probably need that luck."

Two weeks later Caroline whirled in her husband's powerful arms to the strains of a waltz. Washington society glittered around them. The huge ballroom was resplendent with silks and satins, jewels both paste and real, bright chatter and serious dealing. Intermingled with the formal black, gray and midnight-blue tuxedos of the civilians were the gorgeous dress uniforms of the various branches of the military. Joe looked magnificent in his. Caroline saw more than one set of feminine eyes following him wherever he went, and she had been forced to glare several of the owners of those eyes into submission.

"We should have waited," she said.

"For what?" His arm tightened around her as he swung her around.

"To get married."

"For God's sake, why?"

"For your family."

He laughed aloud. "Dad understood. When he decided to marry Mary, he had the deed done within two days. It took me three."

"General Ramey seemed pleased," she commented.

"He is. The Air Force likes its officers to be married. It makes us more settled."

"Sure," she replied doubtfully. "If going Mach 3 is considered settled."

The funding for Night Wing had been granted by a

wide margin in Congress the day before. Joe had had to testify before the committee, requiring his presence in Washington, and he had categorically refused to be separated from his wife, so Caroline's presence had also been required.

The federal investigation into Help Americans First was ongoing, as was the final phase of testing on the Night Wing project, but the aircraft and laser systems were all functioning perfectly. The damage Cal had done to the computer program had been rectified. And Caroline was slowly beginning to realize what it would mean to her life to be married to a career military officer. When the final testing was completed he would be taking over as wing commander of the 1st Tactical Fighter Wing at Langley AFB in Virginia. She had learned a lot about the military in the ten days they had been married and knew that Joe would be up for his first star after that posting. He was thirty-five years old and would probably make general before he was thirty-seven. She would never admit it to him, because she felt he needed someone who didn't jump every time he issued an order, but sometimes she was a little in awe of his abilities.

He pulled her closer, and the movement of the waltz brought her lower body into firm contact with his. Her gaze flew up to meet his, and she saw his arousal reflected in the glittering blue depths of his eyes.

"I like you in white," he murmured.

"That's good. I wear it a lot." She was wearing it now. Her ball gown was pure, snowy white.

"You look better on white sheets than anyone I know."

"Hmm. I'm going to take flying lessons, so maybe I'll need to have several jumpsuits made in white."

Incredibly, she felt his shoulder tense under her hand. "Flying lessons? Why? If you want to fly, I'll teach you."

She gave him a calm smile. "No. I'd turn you into a trembling wreck if you tried to teach me how to fly, and I'd be ready to kill you. But I need to know, so I'll know something of what it's like for you up there." She figured it was the best way to get over the fear she felt every time he went up. Rather than risk clipping his wings, out of his concern for her, she would grow her own wings.

He still looked uneasy. "Caroline..."

"Joe," she replied firmly, "I'm good at anything I decide to do. Physics, computers, sex. I'll be good at flying, too. And having babies."

He stopped dead in the middle of the dance floor. "Caroline!"

She lifted her brows, ignoring the smiling glances directed their way. "What?"

"Are you pregnant?"

"It's possible," she said serenely. "The timing wasn't right during our weekend in Vegas, but what about since then? Name one time when you used any protection. If I'm not now, the odds are good I will be before the end of the year."

He couldn't seem to breathe. Hell, she probably was

pregnant. As she had said, she was very good at anything she decided to do, and so was he.

"It'll be interesting," she said, "to find out if you make girl babies or boy babies."

A slow grin moved his hard, beautiful mouth. "As long as I make you, I'm happy."

"Oh, you do make me, Colonel Mackenzie. Very well indeed. When are we going to Wyoming?"

He adjusted to her lightning change of subject without a pause and resumed the dance. "Next month. I'll only have a week, but we'll get back for Christmas."

"Good. I've talked to Boling-Wahl, and they'll try to keep me assigned to projects in your general vicinity, though of course I won't be working on any project for the Air Force. I may be working in Baltimore while you're at Langley, but the commute isn't bad."

"Not bad," he said doubtfully, "but I don't really like the idea of you having to battle that traffic."

She pulled back a little and her brows slowly rose. "Me?" she asked after a delicate pause.

He stifled a shout of laughter. "I have to be closer to the base than that," he explained, keeping his voice level with an effort.

"Oh." She considered the situation for a moment, then said, "Okay, I'll do it this time. But you owe me, big time, because I believe in being comfortable, and fighting the traffic violates that belief. I'll let you know when I think of some way you can make it up to me."

He tugged her closer, still fighting laughter as he savored the feel of her in his arms. "Mary's going to love you," he said under his breath.

* * *

Mary did love her.

The two women were immediate friends, sensing a basic likeness in each other. Caroline fell in love, not only with his family but with Ruth, Wyoming and the prosperous horse ranch on top of Mackenzie's Mountain. The place was beautiful, and the ranch house was one of the most cheerful places she'd ever been in her life.

Mary Mackenzie was a slight, delicately formed woman with soft blue-gray eyes, pale brown hair and the most exquisite complexion in the world. At first sight she struck Caroline as rather plain, but by day's end her gaze had accustomed itself to the glowing purity of Mary's features and she thought her mother-in-law incredibly beautiful. Certainly Wolf Mackenzie thought his wife was beautiful, if the obvious love and lust in his black eyes every time he looked at her were anything to go by.

She had never seen two men more alike than Joe and his father, the only real difference being that Wolf's eyes were as black as night while Joe's were that brilliant, diamond blue. And looking at Wolf, she could easily understand why Joe had thought his father would kill the man who had abused him, if he had known about it. Wolf Mackenzie protected his own. Like his son, he was pure warrior.

Mary was dwarfed by her sons, even thirteen-year-old Zane, the intense one. Michael was off at college; it would be Christmas before she would meet him. But Joshua, at sixteen, was almost as big as Wolf and Joe. Josh was as bright and lighthearted as Zane was dark and quiet, his gaze watchful. The same dangerous intensity that burned in both Joe and Wolf was evident in the boy.

Then there was Maris. At eleven, she was small for her age, with Mary's slight build and exquisitely translucent complexion. Her hair was pale, her eyes as black as Wolf's. She was her father's shadow, her small hands gentling and soothing the fractious horses as well as Wolf's strong ones did.

For the first time Caroline saw Joe with horses, and another element of his character fell into place. He was infinitely patient with them and rode as if he'd been born in the saddle, which he almost had.

She stood at the kitchen window watching him and Wolf and Maris in the corral with a tall black mare who was currently Maris's favorite. Mary came to stand beside her, knowing instinctively who Caroline was watching. "He's wonderful, isn't he?" Mary sighed. "I loved him the first moment I saw him, when he was sixteen. There aren't many men in this world like Joe. He was a man even then, and I mean it in the purest sense of the word. Of course, I'm prejudiced, but you are, too, aren't you?"

"Just looking at him gives me shivers," Caroline admitted dreamily, then caught herself with a laugh. "But don't tell him that. Sometimes he can be very much the colonel. I try to keep him from being *too* commanding."

"Oh, he knows. The thing is, you give him shivers, too. Keeps things nice and balanced. I should know.

His father has been giving me shivers for almost twenty years now. Do you suppose it's inherited?"

"It probably is. Look at Joshua and Zane."

"I know," Mary sighed. "I feel so sorry for all the girls in school. And all those poor girls in college with Michael haven't had time to get used to him, the way the girls he grew up with did. Not that it did them much good."

"Maris will balance it out with the boys."

Through the window she watched Joe lightly vault the fence and start toward the house. Wolf tousled Maris's hair and followed his son, while Maris remained with the mare.

Both men entered the house, their tall, broad-shouldered forms suddenly making the kitchen seem too small. They brought with them the earthy scents of the outdoors, horse and hay and clear fresh air mingled with their own male sweat.

"You two look guilty," Joe observed. "What have you been talking about?"

"Genetics," Caroline replied.

His brows lifted in that characteristic way. She shrugged. "Well, I can't help it. I'm probably going to be very interested in genetics for the next eight and a half months. Do you want to lay odds on whether it's a boy or a girl?"

"Oh, it's a boy," Mary said, her entire face lit with delight. Joe had gone weak at the knees, and Wolf was laughing at his son as he helped him to a chair. "Joe's a Mackenzie, hardly a female sperm to be found. Mackenzies have to work really hard to have daughters. That's why they appreciate them so much."

Epilogue

Mary was absolutely right. John Mackenzie, eight pounds and two ounces, made his debut right on time. His heritage was immediately apparent in the thick black hair, blue eyes and straight black brows of his father. After his birth Caroline slept, and Joe dozed in the chair by her bed, his son lying on his chest and making squeaky little grunting noises. Caroline awakened, her drowsy eyes moving around the room until her gaze lit on the pair by her side. She reached out, first touching her husband's hand and then the tiny hand that lay curled on his chest.

Joe's eyes opened. "Hi," he said softly.

"Hi, yourself." He looked wonderful, she thought. Kind of grubby and rumpled. He was still in uniform, having been summoned straight from the base. The nurses were probably all swooning at his feet. She grabbed his tie and pulled him closer. "Give me a kiss."

He did, his mouth lingering hungrily over hers. "In a few weeks I'll give you a lot more."

"Umm. I can't wait." He made a few lascivious promises to her that made her heart pound, and she laughed as she took the sleeping baby from him. "You shouldn't talk like that in front of him. He's too young."

"It's nothing new to him, sweetheart. He's been well acquainted with me from the very beginning."

She looked down at the tiny, serious face, and this time her heart swelled, blooming until it nearly filled her chest. It was incredible. This magnificent little creature was incredible. Her parents, having decided to stay in Greece for a couple of years, were on their way, but the flight was so long and the connections so horrible that it would be another ten hours before they arrived. John's other grandparents, however, had managed to get there before he was born, and he'd already been in their arms.

"Where are Wolf and Mary?" she asked sleepily.

"In the cafeteria. They said they were hungry, but I think they wanted to give us some time alone."

"I wish they'd brought Maris and the boys."

"They were taking final exams at school. They'll see him soon enough."

She looked back down at the baby, tracing the downy cheek with her fingertip. To her surprise, he abruptly turned his head toward the touch, the tiny mouth opening as he sought it.

Joe laughed and said, "That isn't it, son. You need to fine-tune your targeting a little."

The baby had begun fretting. Caroline opened her gown and gently guided the avid little mouth to her breast. He clamped down on it with a grunting noise.

"He's a typical Mackenzie," she murmured. "Which means he isn't typical at all."

She looked up and met Joe's eyes, brilliant and filled with more desire and love than she'd ever thought to see in her life. No, there was nothing typical about this man. He was on a fast track to the stars, and he was carrying her with him.

* * * * *

your romantic
books